REMO COULDN'T MAKE LOVE . . .

not to the 200-pound Sinanju siren, Poo, whom Chiun had browbeaten and blackmailed him into marrying.

REMO COULDN'T MAKE WAR . . .

not against an infernal adversary like the mocking Mr. Arieson, whom Chiun himself acknowledged as his equal. Mr. Arieson had a way of disappearing in a cloud of dust every time Remo tried to total him, only to reappear and beat Remo once again at his own Destroyer game.

Remo couldn't make love . . . he couldn't make war . . . and the world couldn't make it to tomorrow unless he did something fast.

What should he do? Hell only knew—and Hell was laughing. . . .

—— THE DESTROYER #68 ——
AN OLD-FASHIONED WAR

#68

The Destroyer

AN OLD-FASHIONED WAR

WARREN MURPHY & RICHARD SAPIR

A SIGNET BOOK

NEW AMERICAN LIBRARY

PUBLISHER'S NOTE

This book is a work of fiction. Names, characters, places, and incidents either are the product of the author's imagination or are used fictitiously, and any resemblance to actual persons, living or dead, events, or locales is entirely coincidental.

SIGNET TRADEMARK REG. U.S. PAT. OFF. AND FOREIGN COUNTRIES
REGISTERED TRADEMARK—MARCA REGISTRADA
HECHO EN CHICAGO, U.S.A.

SIGNET, SIGNET CLASSIC, MENTOR, ONYX, PLUME, MERIDIAN and NAL BOOKS are published by NAL PENGUIN INC., 1633 Broadway, New York, New York 10019

First Printing, April, 1987

1 2 3 4 5 6 7 8 9

PRINTED IN THE UNITED STATES OF AMERICA

He was going to die. If he stayed in Chicago one more day, he knew he would go to the top of one of the taller buildings and throw himself off, or maybe look into the barrel of the .45-caliber pistol his brother had brought home from Vietnam and test-fire it into his own forehead. He thought of trains, but trains might leave him only mangled. Trains weren't a sure thing. Trains were fickle as fate, and Bill Buffalo knew many poems about fate. He thought of fate as a person, a god, a muse, a force personified in cadences as strange to the English language as his native Ojupa language, now officially declared a dead tongue of historical interest alone. He was an Ojupa brave. He was born to hunt. To run. To dance around fires at night, and look into his own soul through the animals of the American plains.

The only animals in his tenement flat were mice, possibly rats, and of course roaches. And the only thing he wanted to dance about was death, his own.

With a slow deliberate motion, he put the clip of .45-caliber slugs into the automatic and looked down the barrel of the gun. What a last vision, he thought. A white man's tool.

"What are you doing in there?" called his landlady. She always called out when his door was shut.

"I'm going to blow my brains out," yelled Bill Buffalo.

"All right, but don't damage the wallpaper," she replied.

"I can't promise that," said Bill Buffalo.

"Why not?" asked the landlady, pushing open the door.

"Because I'll be dead. The dead don't clean up after themselves," said Bill Buffalo.

"Oh my—" said the landlady, seeing the young student sitting in his shorts at the edge of the brand-new bed, a large pistol pointed at his head, and his thumb about to pull the trigger. Immediately she understood the danger. If he missed, the slug would go directly into the new rose-patterned wallpaper behind him. It was from a remnants sale and there was no way she could replace it. Put a hole in the paper, and she would either have to cover it with some picture, or if that failed, buy entirely new paper for the wall and maybe the whole room.

"Don't shoot," she cried. "You've got so much to live for."

"What?" asked Bill Buffalo.

"Lots of things," she said. Her name was Tracto. Because of her bulk people called her Tractor, but never to her face.

"What?"

"Me," she said. She tried to smile at him lasciviously. When she first rented to him she had been afraid of rape. She would watch him walk down the hall, his beautifully muscled body clad in just a pair of shorts, and she would lock her door so that he couldn't walk in and take her forcibly. Then she stopped locking her door and then started leaving it ajar and going to sleep half-nude. And still her fears weren't realized. Now she told herself she could save the handsome young Indian with her body. If it was to save a life, it would not be a sin.

"What do you mean, you?" said Bill Buffalo.

"I would give my body to save your life," said Angela Tracto.

"I don't need body organs. I don't want body organs. I want to die."

"I meant sexually," said Angela Tracto, lowering her eyes.

She saw his thumb tighten on the trigger and his eyes go wide, waiting for the slug.

"And there are other things," she cried.

"What?"

"Don't you want to say good-bye to your friends back in Ojupa land?"

"There is no Ojupa land, only the reservation."

"But you do have friends."

"I have friends," said Bill Buffalo sadly. "I have Indian friends and I have white friends. And I have no friends. Do you know what you get for studying three years of nothing but classical Greek literature?"

"A degree?"

"You get crazy. I don't know whether I'm an Indian or a white man. Dammit, I think more like an ancient Greek than I do an Ojupa or an American white. I'm nothing, and the place for nothing is death."

"Something must have brought this on," said Angela Tracto. If she could get him to turn around, then maybe the bullet would hit a window. She had a renter's policy from a mail-order catalog. The windows were insured. The wallpaper was not. Also insured were doors, chandeliers, and moats that had to be redredged in case of siege. Wallpaper, floors, and fire damage were not. But that was all right. What could one expect for pennies a month? If the

Phrygians ever raided South Chicago, Angela Tracto would be rich.

"My brother died. He got drunk and he drove a tractor into a ditch and it turned over on him. It crushed him. And I didn't go to the funeral."

"Well, there's nothing you can do for the dead. Do you want to turn around a bit?"

"It's not his death that made me sad. It's not that I did not go to the funeral that made me sad. What made me realize *I* was dead was when my father chanted the death dirge over the telephone, and do you know what I did?"

"You asked him if the call was collect?"

"I didn't know Ojupa from Greek or Latin. I didn't know it. I didn't know the words for 'mother' or 'father' or 'earth' or 'good-bye.' I had forgotten the words. And I answered my own father with a quote from Sophocles."

Bill Buffalo took a very deep breath and then shut his eyes because he had decided finally he did not want to see the bullet.

"You can learn to be Indian again. Don't pull the trigger. You can learn again."

"It's too late."

"How did you learn the first time?"

"The first time I didn't have all these other languages swimming around in my head. The first time I didn't dream in Greek or Latin. The first time all I knew was Ojupa."

"You can do it again. Lots have done it. I've had many young men who went to the big university and felt just the way you do, and when they returned to their home countries, everything was fine. Their problem was they were here. Like you. Just get up and face another direction and you'll feel better. Try it."

Bill Buffalo looked at the big barrel. He was sure

he wouldn't feel a thing, and that was what he was after: not feeling. On the other hand, why not get up and see if he felt better?

He lowered the gun. Ms. Tracto must have been very happy at that because a big grin spread over her face. That was strange. He never thought she cared about anything but the rent or possibly getting him into her bedroom, the door of which always seemed to be open at night.

"There, see. Don't that feel better?"

"Feels pretty much like before," said Bill Buffalo.

"That's because you're not home. Go home. Go back to the reservation. You'll see."

"I don't belong there."

"That's how you feel now. Not how you'll feel when you're there. Trust me. I know."

It was a lie, of course, but a successful wallpaper-saving lie. What Angela Tracto didn't know was that she was sending back to Ojupa, Oklahoma, the man whose birth all mankind would regret and who might possibly bring about the end of the world.

If she had been told that a scourge as old as the first raising of one brother's hand against another was going to reappear, she would have said so long as it didn't reappear on her rose wallpaper that was all right with her. But then, she didn't know what the handsome young man with the strong cheek-bones had studied. She didn't know the ancient texts and she didn't know how Greek would combine with Ojupa one night around a fire, when this young man, this walking H-bomb, returned to Oklahoma to be reunited with his people.

All she knew was that her rose wallpaper was safe.

"I never thought you knew that much about human behavior," said Bill Buffalo, putting down the gun. "I never figured you for that."

By the next morning he was in Ojupa, Oklahoma, with the heat and the dust and the shanties with the television antennas and the bottles of whiskey and beer lying in open sewers, some of the bottles still attached to his relatives. In Ojupa it was absolutely clear again why he had left: no future. And for him not even much of a past.

"Hey, Bill fella, good to see you back, man," said Running Deere. Running Deere was named after a tractor because everyone knew a tractor was more reliable than any animal. Besides, real deer hadn't run around the Ojupa lands for decades now, but John Deere tractors almost always seemed to run.

"I've come home," said Bill Buffalo.

"How's life in the big city?" asked Running Deere, hoisting his balloon paunch over his too-tight Levi's. He wore a T-shirt proclaiming his love for Enid, Oklahoma.

"I want to get away from it. I want to get away from everything I learned there. I don't know who I am anymore. I'm going to visit my brother's grave. I'm going to sing the death chant. Would you come with me, Running Deere? Would you bring others who know the Ojupa tongue? Would you bring the medicine man?"

"You sure you don't want a beer first?"

"I don't want beer. I don't want whiskey. I don't want tractors. I want Ojupa ways. I don't even want these white man's clothes."

"Hey, if you don't want those cool jeans, I'll take them," said Running Deere.

"You can have everything. Just chant with me at my brother's grave and don't forget the medicine man and Little Elk, and my father. And never again call me Bill, but Big Buffalo," said Bill.

That night he put on clothes that felt right and

natural, leaving his legs and arms free, not bound, and gave up his shirt and jeans and went with the friends of his childhood to his brother's grave, and there in the full Oklahoma moon he joined those of his blood in reverence for one of the tribe who had gone to join those who no longer lived in this world.

The night was cold and his skin prickled with goose bumps, but he didn't mind as he felt the old chants come back to him. Warm as his mother's milk, familiar as a hug, the words came from the back of his throat, dancing on his tongue, clicking at his teeth as though he had never forgotten them. All the Chicago boarding rooms and all the hours of study in the library were gone as he felt his feet join with the earth and himself become one with his people. It had worked. Ms. Tracto, the landlady, was right. He was home, and he would never leave again. The words poured out, about loss, about return, until, totally one with the Ojupa words themselves, he said:

"Atque in perpetuum frater, ave atque valle."

And smiling he turned to his tribesmen, to see their faces blank and the medicine man, normally the last to show any emotion on his withered seventy-year-old-face, shocked. His tribesmen looked at each other in confusion.

"What's wrong?" he asked.

"What language you speaking, Big Buffalo?"

"Ojupa. It was beautiful. I said to my brother, 'And so, brother, forever, hello and good-bye.' "

"That ain't Ojupa, never has been," said Running Deere.

The medicine man, in his feathers and sacred paint, shook his head.

"But the words came right from my soul," said Big Buffalo. "It's the most famous Ojupa saying. Hello and good-bye. It's from a poem about a young man who returns from abroad and finds his brother dead, and says, 'And so, brother, forever, hello and good-bye.' Ave atque valle."

Big Buffalo slapped his forehead and groaned. He had just recited a Latin poem from Catullus. The "abroad" he had referred to was the other end of the long-dead Roman Empire.

He fell to his knees before the medicine man.

"Save me. Save me. Kill the foreign spirits in me. Rid me of the white man's curse. I don't want his education. I don't want his languages. I want to dream in my people's tongues."

But the medicine man shook his head.

"This I cannot do," he said sadly. "There is only one way to rid you of the curse, and it is the most ancient and dangerous ceremony of our heritage."

"I don't mind dying. I'm already dead," said Big Buffalo.

"It's not your death I fear," said the medicine man.

"Hey, give the guy what he wants," said Running Deere. He had always liked Big Buffalo and felt the medicine man too much a stickler for the old ways. Besides, there weren't that many old ways left, considering the television and booze and pickup trucks that had become the real life of the Ojupa tribe.

But the medicine man shook his head. They were on sacred ground, the small hill that held the remains of those who had passed on to the other world of the Ojupa. It had been made sacred by the buffalo horns and the fires of the dried mushrooms, and the grasses of the plains and the good spirits that had been called here by previous medicine men. There were crosses here too, because some Ojupa were Christians. But it was still sacred ground because the medicine men of the tribe had prepared it first. The war dead were here also, those who had fought against the white man's cavalry and those who, in later wars, for the white men against other white men. There were marines and soldiers here as well as braves.

"Hey, medicine man, why you shaking your head?" asked Little Elk. He was a construction worker in nearby Enid and he was big enough to stick the old man under an arm and carry him around like a parcel.

"Big Buffalo's problems are bad. There are tales of a man who has lost the soul of his people. This is not new. But the whole tribe must ask the spirits to visit if he is to be saved."

"Okay. You're always doin' that stuff with spirits and things."

"There are spirits and there are spirits. These are the spirits of blood and anger and pride and the great spirit of misjudgment."

"Misjudgment?" asked Little Elk. He laughed. He had never heard of that one and it didn't sound too frightening. Besides, they were running out of beer, and the cemetery on the hill gave him the willies. He didn't like any cemetery, especially at night. Big Buffalo, who had been the smartest kid at the reservation school, was crying on his knees, his hands up in the air, babbling that strange foreign language. Running Deere was looking at his watch because he knew the liquor store was closing soon in nearby Enid, and the others were slapping their arms because the Oklahoma night was getting very cold.

The stars looked brighter on a cold night, thought Little Elk. He hated stars. He hated anything having to do with the outdoors. He hated loud noises. Little Elk liked computers and air-conditioned rooms and people who never raised their voices. Running Deere was yelling at the medicine man and Big Buffalo was crying, and finally Little Elk said:

"Medicine man, do the prayers. Say the chants. C'mon. It's late. It's cold. Big Buffalo has always been a nice guy. One of the nicest. Give him a break. And give me a break too. And the rest of us."

"Yeah," said Running Deere.

And the others joined in too, so that the medicine man finally and wearily said, "I am old. I will not have to live with what happens, but you will, all of you."

"Hey, medicine man, nothing ever happens. If our medicine is so strong, what are we doing in a stinking patch of ground the white man left us? Just do it, make Big Buffalo happy, and let's get out of here and get a drink." Thus spoke Little Elk, but he spoke for all of them.

The old man lowered himself to his knees, and stretched out his arms, palms upward, and began to chant, earth tones with the rhythm of the earth, sky tones with the rhythms of the universe sparkling above them on the little cemetery hill of Ojupa land. Big Buffalo joined the chant with his funny language. Running Deere felt an urge to build a fire, and Little Elk, who normally hated anything physical, scurried around gathering twigs for the fire. The medicine man lowered his head to the earth, and reaching into his waistband withdrew a handful of sacred mushrooms.

He dropped them into the fire, and the fire smoked and they gathered around the little blaze and breathed in the sacred smoke and exhaled the chants, the medicine man and the young braves in the Ojupa tongue and poor Big Buffalo in the crazy language.

The smoke grew and danced, and stretched its arms, and howled, a long, low howl deeper than a coyote and stronger than a bear. Iron banged against iron, and cries of the wounded filled the night air, even though they all knew no one around them had been hurt and no one was banging anything. Big Buffalo was laughing and Little Elk was screaming when they heard the first words.

Later each would recall that the words came in the language he was most comfortable with.

They would wonder what language Big Buffalo heard that night, but they would never know.

"You look like a bunch of regular guys with some brains and guts," came the voice from the fire. There was a man in the fire. He was laughing. Even in his suit, everyone could see he was well built. He looked like a man of men, with a clean smile, a strong jaw, and eyes that seemed to shine in the night.

He carried a briefcase. He didn't burn. The briefcase didn't burn, and the fire went out suddenly, as though doused by a passing rainstorm. But it wasn't raining.

"Hey, let's get a drink," he said. "Let's have some fun."

"Liquor store is closed," said Little Elk. "I knew we wouldn't make it."

"Closed. Fine young men like yourselves denied drink? Who closed it?" asked the man. He thumped his chest, inhaling the good night air.

"It's a liquor store. State runs it. Sells liquor by the bottle. It's closed," said Little Elk.

"Which state?"

"Oklahoma. You're in Oklahoma, mister. I didn't get your name," said Running Deere.

"Whatever you want to call me, friend. I'm here for you. I'm going to make you rich, respected, and famous. I'm going to make you feel like real men. I'm going to make it so that when they sing songs around your campfires a thousand years from today they will remember your names with awe. That's who I am."

"And you call yourself?"

"Liquor store. Are you going to let Oklahoma tell you when you can drink and when you can't? Slaves live like that. Are you slaves?"

"It's closed, mister," said Little Elk. "We missed it."

"Whose locks? Who has a right to lock you out on land that should be your own? Free men, real men, own their land. What are you?"

"Who are you?" asked Running Deere.

"The man who's going to get you some fine drink, the sort of liquor you deserve whenever you want it. Not when Oklahoma tells you."

"I don't know," said Running Deere.

"A big man like yourself? What are you afraid of?"

They didn't know his name, but they knew he made sense. This muscular stranger who had appeared out of the fire had an answer for everything. No one noticed, as they marched off the little hill of the cemetery, that the medicine man was not with them. His head was still pressed to the ground, and he was crying, crying that the wrong spirit had been unleashed. Nor did they notice Big Buffalo in a trance, saying nothing, his eyes wide, mumbling only the funny tongue he had learned at the white man's school in Chicago.

At the edge of the cemetery the man turned and threw a snappy salute at the graves.

"I like war dead," he said. "Lets you know men lived here. Real men. The Ojupa are great among peoples. Never let anyone tell you otherwise. You hear?"

They still didn't know his name when they drove

into Enid in a pickup truck. The liquor store was locked and barred, and the streets were empty.

"Never getting in," said Little Elk.

"I could tell you how to get in there, but a smart guy like you, Little Elk, can figure it out," said the stranger, giving Little Elk a manly slap on the back. "It's an adventure. Let's go for it."

The man's corporate gray suit never seemed to wrinkle and his tie was as neat as he when he stepped out of the smoke of the campfire back at the Ojupa cemetery. The braves felt a sense of excitement about this man, more than anything they had ever felt in sports, more than in the biggest football game.

"What have you got to lose?" he asked. "You want me to lead? I'll lead." He jumped out of the truck, but not before Running Deere, who now seemed faster than ever, cut him off and headed for the front door. Little Elk figured the rear would be easier, and with a car jack he pried open the bars at the rear of the store. Alarms went off but Running Deere and the stranger were too fast. They were in the store and out with a case of whiskey apiece before any police could arrive, and the pickup truck sped out of Enid with everyone singing old Ojupa war songs. By morning, everyone but the stranger had a hangover, and they could see sheriff's cars crisscrossing the reservation looking for them.

"How did they find out it was us?" asked Little Elk.

"I told them," said the stranger happily. He looked even healthier in the daylight, with bright eyes, a peppy disposition, and a can-do attitude. Running Deere wanted to throttle the man. But Big Buffalo, who had found them and who was still mouthing that funny language, reverted to English to tell them not to bother, that it wouldn't do any good.

"I'll tell you the good it'll do, Bill. It'll make me feel good when I go off to jail," said Running Deere.

"And me too," said Little Elk. And so did the others. But the stranger only grinned at the threats.

"Shoot me. Go ahead. Shoot me," he said. "If there is anyone here who loves the Ojupa more than I, let him blow my brains out now. Go ahead."

"You call bringing the sheriff's office down on us an act of love?" asked Little Elk.

"I couldn't have given you a greater gift. Because after today, you will never skulk around a sheriff again. You will never fear when you see his blue bubble coming after you on a highway, or hear his siren. You are meant to walk on this Ojupa land as lords of it, not frightened little boys. Are you men or boys? As for me, give me liberty or give me death."

The stranger snapped open his case and there inside were five brand-new mini-machine guns, smaller than the famed Israeli Uzi, hardly larger than pistols.

"The question is, do you guys want to live forever? Or are you going to stand up once for manhood? Are you going to honor those dead in your cemetery, or are you going to go on living like half Indians, half whites, all nothing? As for me, death doesn't frighten me nearly as much as slavery, nearly as much as seeing my women look down on me, nearly as much as living each dusty, dreary day like some little gopher who has to hide at the sound of a footstep. I cannot promise you victory this day, good Ojupa braves, but I can promise you honor. And that is all any of us have in the end."

There wasn't a shaking hand in the band as they reached for the submachine guns. And it was known throughout the reservation and indeed on other reservations and across the country what happened that day. A handful of Ojupa braves annihilated an entire sheriff's posse, and when the state troopers were sent in, they took them on too. They flew the banner of the Ojupa, and Running Deere said it best for all of them:

"Maybe we won't win this day, and maybe we won't live this day, but the world will sure as hell know we were here."

The state troopers had automatic weapons too, and even an armored car. They outnumbered the small band and had all been trained to a fine edge. But there was a spirit now in the Ojupa. Little Elk didn't mind discomfort and Running Deere no longer waddled but moved swiftly.

They fought through the morning and into the afternoon and laughed at requests to surrender, scoffed at warnings that their cause was hopeless, and by nightfall other young men had joined them.

In a brilliant night attack devised by Little Elk and led by Running Deere, the now larger band outflanked the state troopers and forced them to surrender, taking all their weapons.

"We'll let you live so that you may tell others that you have met the real Ojupa," said Running Deere. He no longer wore blue jeans or a shirt that professed love for Enid, Oklahoma, but a uniform made of real deerskin. A knife was stuck in his belt.

"When we come back we will fill the sky with so many helicopters we'll block out the damned sun," said a state trooper, angry that they should yield to an outlaw band.

"Then we will fight in the shade," said Running Deere.

His words and the deeds of the Ojupa spread to other reservations. By the time the reinforced state troopers returned, they were met by a little army composed of frustrated, downtrodden braves, and this time the army outnumbered the troopers.

And Little Elk, warned about helicopters, had prepared defenses against the slow-moving targets with the many guns. The state troopers fought bravely that day, but the Ojupa were braver and shrewder.

Many died, but as the stranger said, "The tree of liberty is watered with the blood of patriots."

They buried their dead, even as warnings that the Oklahoma National Guard were about to close in came to the little cemetery on the hill.

One of the dead was Big Buffalo, or Bill Buffalo as he was known for a while. He was buried with full honors, even though it didn't seem as though he died in battle. There were powder burns at his right temple and a gun was found in his right hand. One of the braves remembered his last words.

Big Bill Buffalo had kept repeating:

"Tu cogno, tu cogno."

No one knew what it meant, until later, when it was all over, one of Buffalo's teachers from Chicago came down to pay last respects to one of his finest students ever.

"Who was he talking to?" asked the teacher.

"Wasn't talking to anyone. He was looking at our friend who came out of the campfire, and just kept saying those funny words. He said them and then put the gun to his head. And bang. Pulled the trigger," said the witness.

"His words are Latin. And they mean 'I know you. You I know.' "

"Well, shoot," said one of the other braves, listening in. "That's good. 'Cause no one else here knows him."

With the leadership of the stranger and their own good fighting skills and courage, the Ojupa that day registered the first Indian victory against federal troops since the Battle of Little Big Horn. But by now other tribes were ready to join, because this time the word was in the air:

"This time we can win."

In Washington the news was grim. An entire National Guard division, one of the best in the country with the most modern equipment, had been soundly defeated in Oklahoma. Not only that, but the Indian band was growing daily as it marched northward. It had to be stopped.

The problem was that it would be Americans fighting Americans.

"If we win, we still lose," said the President.

"We've got to find a way to stop this without a war," said the Secretary of the Interior.

"If you could increase our budget," began the Secretary of Defense.

"What on earth is left for you to buy?" snapped the President, astonished that the Defense Department still wanted to spend more money even though every month it went through the gross national product of most of the rest of the world.

"We could form an exploratory purchase committee to look for new technology."

"We have enough technology. We need a quiet victory without a battle," said the President.

"Impossible. Those things don't exist," said the Secretary of the Interior.

"We could buy one," said the Secretary of Defense.

"From whom?" asked the President. He was known to the public as an amiable person, not concerned with details. But every cabinet member knew he had a firm, sharp grasp of facts, and while he never became angry in front of television cameras, he certainly could show anger in these meetings.

There was silence among the cabinet.

"Thank you, gentlemen. That's all I want to know," he said, dismissing them. Then he went to the bedroom in the White House and, at the proper time, took a red telephone out of a bureau drawer. He did not have to dial. As soon as he picked up the phone it would ring. This time he did not hear the reassuring voice saying that everything would be taken care of, that there was no wall that posed an obstacle or killer elite that was a threat. This time, reaching out for America's most powerful and most secret enforcing arm, he got a wrong number.

2

His name was Remo and there was no reason he couldn't handle a simple telephone connection as well as the next guy. It was just a matter of putting one connector into another. That it had to be done by getting past guard dogs, and over one of the most modern defense perimeters in the world, did not matter. It was still a simple connection.

"You plug the red socket into the red receptacle. We've colored it red so you won't forget," Harold W. Smith had told him.

There had been a problem on the direct-access line from the White House and Smith feared that the President might not be able to get through without being compromised by some new electronic device on sale to the public. There was so much electronics out there, private eavesdropping, that it had become a problem for the organization to keep its secret phone calls secret. The very office of the presidency could be ruined if ever it was discovered an organization so contrary to the laws of the country was being used to protect those very same laws. There would be disaster if others than the small group that comprised it should ever know of its existence.

Therefore more secure phone access was called for.

As Harold W. Smith, the lemon-faced head of the organization, explained it, Remo should imagine sound waves as two giant pillows encapsulating the world. America's eavesdropping and Russia's. Where they met created an absolutely perfect interference pattern. If the organization could establish its sending base inside that area by the simple plugging of one cord into a monitoring station there, then the President could use his red phone without fear of anyone listening in.

The problem was that the monitoring station was in Cuba, right smack in its most heavily fortified area, just outside the American base at Guantánamo. There the Cuban special forces practiced approaching the American defenses and then retreating. To penetrate the monitoring station to repair the phone lines in the overlap area would be like swimming through a tide of oncoming humans, the best-trained humans in Cuba.

"Let me get this straight," Remo had said. "The red plug into the red socket."

Smith nodded. They were on a small patrol boat just off the coast of Florida. They would meet, if everything went well, in Puerto Rico after the assignment. Even though it was sweltering, Smith still wore his gray three-piece suit.

"And the blue wire into the blue connector. We know the Russian connector is blue. They always coat their connectors in that sort of installation with blue. It's a special noncorrosive metal. Everything tends to corrode in the Caribbean. The Russians have placed their station over an old American monitoring station. Don't worry about the electronics. It will work. Just get into the station with the equipment. And then get out without them knowing you were ever there. That's the problem. We're piggybacking this thing. They've got to think everything is running normally. Can you do it?"

"Red into red," said Remo.

"Getting in and out without being seen, through a wave of their special forces?"

"And blue into blue," said Remo. He looked at the blue wire. Nothing special, no longer than nine inches, with a tiny electrode attached. And the red plug seemed just like a simple outlet plug. He held both of them in one hand.

"Through a wave of their special forces without them knowing you were ever there," repeated Smith.

"Red into red. Blue into blue. Should be easy," Remo had said.

"If they know you've been there, the whole thing is blown," said Smith.

"I'll put the red one in first," said Remo.

And he kept that in mind as he waited for dusk to slip into a little gully just beneath a marine machine gun nest at the outer rim of the Guantánamo naval base. He could have told the marines a friend was going to move through their lines, but their help would probably only serve to alert the other side.

It wasn't full dark as his soft steps became softer, not pressing on the earth but becoming a friend with the ground underneath, feeling the rhythms of the humid Caribbean air, the silence of the ground, the moisture on his skin, and the rich smell of the green jungle growth all around him.

He wasn't a man sneaking past some marines, he was part of the environment they worked in. He was the air they felt, the ground they walked on, the sounds of the jungle, part of it all. And being part, they didn't see him. One sergeant thought he had seen a shadow pass, but shadows, especially at dusk, were everywhere. What they did hear was the rustle beyond of another Cuban special-forces battalion starting their advance.

They would come close, as though attacking, so close they could make out faces even with little light, and then at the last minute they would retreat.

This evening the jungle hummed as fifteen hundred Cubans moved as silently as they could toward the American perimeter. They moved forward and they moved back, and through them moved a man who blended into the jungle more completely than any of the animals living there. And they finished their exercise never knowing that the man had simply walked by them.

Remo found the monitoring station as he was told he would, where he was told he would, and he easily located the guards through their movements. He was quiet within himself, the sort of quiet that does not listen for sounds but allows the body not to strain, thus doing more than not making sounds, becoming the silence that makes all other sound, no matter how small, clear. Through the noise he knew where the guards were, how quickly they walked, or, if they sat, by their breathing how awake they were. And he simply moved where they weren't.

And he found the right room, and he found the red socket. And everything would have gone perfectly, except there was a red wire near the red socket. And Smith had not told him about the red wire.

"Don't panic," he told himself. He plugged the red socket into the red plug. His lean body and sharp features seemed to blend into the darkness even of the machines of the installation. Only his thick wrists seemed to stand out, poking from a dark body-tight shirt set above dark gray slacks. He wore loafers because he never liked shoes tight to his feet. They interrupted the sensitivity of his soles.

The red plug looked fine. He heard one of the guards move down a nearby corridor. He was approaching the room. Blue wire. Remo looked for the blue wire in the machine Smith had described. He found it. Blue wire to blue wire. He attached the blue wire.

Done. He had done it. But why was everything sparking? And why was he hearing some woman in Omaha speaking to the President of the United States? At least it sounded like the President.

"Smith? Is that you?"

"I'm sorry, this is Marion Kilston. I'm from the Omaha Neighbors Bureau. I'm offering today a new introductory neighbor-acquaintance kit."

"Not Smith?"

"We don't have a Smith, although you would think we would, it's such a common name, don't you think? Who is this? You sound just like the President."

The line went dead. Remo pulled out the red plug and saw the brass prongs were twisted. Apparently they didn't fit into the socket. He looked again. It wasn't a socket. It was red, but it wasn't a socket. It had Russian writing on it. It looked like a socket. It was sort of round. But it wasn't a socket.

The problem was that when you used the human body to its cosmic correctness you unleashed the awesome powers of the mind through the universe. Speed and power became something else again. They became knowledge. That was what all training was about, for the body and the mind to know. Unfortunately, when one had difficulty with electrical gadgets, or for that matter any gadgets from toasters to garlic presses, this power left one with plugs that looked like brass taffy. If killing a Russian who had put that sign on the monitor that looked very much like a socket would have helped, Remo would have been fine, he thought. Two Russians or ten would have been fine. Unfortunately, there were no Russians about, and doing harm wouldn't have done much good in the first place. And then Remo noticed two dark vertical slits in a small reddish piece of plastic at the top of the machine. The socket!

Remo took the crushed brass mass at the end of the socket between his two fingers, and slowly, more slowly than more people could perceive, he let his fingers understand the brass, sense the soft yellowish metal, moving its parts ever so slowly, building the heat within it, rubbing, and then faster, so that his fingers could hardly be seen rubbing the yellow metal into a sticky goo, which he flattened and molded and remade into brass prongs as it hardened just so.

"There," muttered Remo, and with a flourish pushed it right into the real socket and there were no sparks. It was in. He had done it. By himself.

Hard leather scuffed on concrete floors. The guard's hand was on the trigger behind Remo, and while Remo wanted to stay and admire his work—he was sure the connection was correct, and so proud he'd gotten it right—if he let the guard get off a shot, one of the bullets could land in the machinery, leaving his connection useless. Also, he was supposed to make sure he was never known to have been in there.

He didn't jump backward but let his body fall backward, so that it didn't look as though he were jumping from his feet but actually pulled into the guard. The motion was deceptive. The guard saw the man with his back to him, leveled the gun before ordering the intruder to throw up his hands.

And then the intruder was on him with the guard's gun flung up above his head, and something apparently slow but fast enough to cause incredible pain, landing hard in the guard's midsection and cutting through his spinal column, and the world went black.

Remo trundled the guard and his gun out of the room toward the next guard post, where, holding the guard's wrists, he started a fight with another guard, keeping himself behind the corpse's body. Slap, punch. The old way of fighting. Remo moved the dead guard's hands in front of the living one, keeping that guard confused, getting that guard to fight, and then he pulled the trigger once, and threw the body at the living struggling guard, knocking him down, and letting him fight his way free of the corpse. They would report the dead one had gone berserk and the living one had fought him off and killed him. The shot, of course, would attract others and there would be confusion, and no one would ever think that the monitor room with the perfect, beautiful plug placed exactly in the socket was ever entered by an American.

What people wanted when they investigated something was an answer. It didn't have to be the correct answer. In large organizations like armies it only had to be an acceptable answer. No one was going to believe that someone in the people's-liberation-monitoring station had started a fight using a corpse, and then escaped without being seen. It was far simpler to believe one guard was forced to subdue another and in the process killed him. That the loser suffered a displaced spinal disk would be glossed over.

That would raise questions. And armies never even answered questions, much less asked them.

Thus Remo remembered from his lessons the wisdom about armies as he moved into the night, out of the monitoring station as though he had never been around. Armies, as it was written in the history of Sinanju, never changed. Only the names and flags were different.

It had been a long time since he had read the histories of Sinanju, Remo thought, coming back through American lines and appearing at a helicopter pad where Smith said transportation would be arranged for him. It had been a long time since his death had been faked so the organization could have a killer arm without fingerprints in any file, a man who would not be missed, an orphan, a dead man for an organization that was not supposed to exist, one man serving as its killer arm. And because there was only one man, he had to be trained in a special way, a way surpassing anything any white man had ever known before.

In that training, he had become something else. He had become Sinanju, the sun source of all understanding of human power, the home of the Masters of Sinanju. In his spirit he was as much that small fishing village on the West Korea Bay as he was Remo Williams, ex-cop, American.

He thought about that as the special helicopter, camouflaged for night, landed at the base helipad. The pilot could be heard telling the commander of the pad that he was to pick someone up, and the commander was arguing back that he had not been told of any such person.

"We're at the tip of Cuba, buddy. No one gets in or out of here without identification," said the commander.

"I'm told he's going to be here."

"By whom?"

"Can't say."

"Yeah, well, you take those CIA or NSA or whatever letters you want to disguise your spies by and stuff 'em somewhere. This place is guarded by U.S. marines. No one gets through."

"Excuse me," said Remo, moving from behind the helipad commander and up into the chopper.

"Are you blue angel zebra?"

"Maybe. Something like that," said Remo. "I don't know."

"You're the one. They said you wouldn't know your code."

"Who's they?" screamed the helipad commander.

"They never say," yelled back the helicopter pilot, taking off into the night. Above, the lights of the fighters keeping protective cover over the fleet and the base competed weakly with the stars.

Remo edged back in his seat and folded his arms and his legs, and went into that quiet place that was his sleep now. He could smell the burning fuel, and even the new rivets in the helicopter, but he focused on the stars and the patches of clean air, and his own blood system. And they were good, all good.

When the helicopter landed, a blood-red dawn was breaking over the Caribbean, exposing the little stucco villas of the Puerto Rican resort Flora del Mar. Remo could make out the golf courses and tennis courts and swimming pools. He guided the pilot toward one small villa set on a canal. Sport-fishing boats with their high captain's nests bobbed along the canal like large white fat gulls grounded in the water.

Remo was out of the helicopter before it fully landed. He walked toward what sounded like a wounded bird squealing softly in a pitch so high that some of the local dogs, dogs looking more like large rodents than canines, were wandering around in a quiet frenzy looking for the source.

Remo knew where it was coming from. He even knew the words. The call was a greeting to the sun, and as he entered the villa, the sounds became louder and then stopped.

"Did you bring the rice?" came the squeaky voice.

"I forgot, Little Father," said Remo. "I was working out this electronics problem."

"Better you should learn Sinanju than wires and bulbs. Leave that for whites and Japanese."

"I am white. Besides, Koreans are getting into electronics now too."

In the living room a wisp of a man with patches of white hair hanging over his ears sadly shook his head. He sat facing the sun in a glorious golden kimono of the dawn, with the precious yellow threads creating designs of splendid mornings over the Korean hills around Sinanju.

"To do one thing well makes a man special. To do one thing better than all others makes one Sinanju. But to be Sinanju means to be in a constant state of becoming, for that which is not moving toward something moves away from it." Thus spoke Chiun, reigning Master of Sinanju, to Remo, who had once been his pupil but was now a Master too.

"I'm not going to read the histories of Sinanju again," said Remo.

"And why not, may I ask?"

"Because I have made the last passage. I'm a Master now. I love you, Little Father. You are the greatest teacher in the world, but I am not reading that nonsense about how Sinanju saved the world from one aeon to the next just because we were paid killers."

"Not killers. Assassins. A bad virus is a killer. An auto accident is a killer. A soldier firing a gun is a killer. But an assassin to a monach is a force for peace and justice."

"How are we a force for justice, Little Father?"

"We get paid and we support the village of Sinanju, full of base ingrates to be sure, but those are our people."

"How is that justice? We go to the higher bidder."

"Would going to the lower bidder be more just?" asked Chiun with a delicious cackle.

"That's what I said. Killers for hire."

"That," said Chiun, "is a dirty lie. If you would read the histories of Sinanju you would see that. But no. You learn the ways of things, but you don't learn the reason of things."

"You think Ivan the Terrible of Russia did justice? He killed people for wearing the wrong clothes."

"Slanderers of his name in your West destroyed his beautiful reputation. He was a most just czar."

"Yeah? How?"

"He paid on time, and paid in good gold. No one in Sinanju ever starved because Ivan the Just failed to pay his Sinanju assassin."

"No one ever starved anyhow. You never used the tributes. They just piled up in that big funny-looking building on the hill. That was just an excuse to hoard more wealth."

"The treasure of Sinanju, hoarding?" Chiun let out a pained cry to the very heavens above this new-world sky. A Master of Sinanju, the white man he had trained, had called the sacred treasure of Sinanju, the earnings of four millennia, a hoard.

"Besides," said Chiun, "it has all been stolen."

"Don't bring up that again. America has more than tripled its gold tribute just to make it up to you."

"It can never be made up to me or the House of Sinanju. While you were out saving the world, a world which has never done anything for you, you let me search alone for the treasure."

"Yeah, well, where would Sinanju be if the world went?" said Remo.

"The world is always coming to an end from one thing or another, so you say. But it always goes on," said Chiun.

"And so does Sinanju," snapped Remo.

"Because we do things right. We honor the treasure. Lost were coins and jewels from Alexander—a white man but definitely great—statues of such fine porcelain, such exquisite craftsmanship that the Ming emperors only gave them to their sons, and of course to us, Sinanju, their house of assassins; gems from the great pharaoh worth entire countries; tributes from all the ages. Gone."

"And what about the American gold that pays for my services to my country?" said Remo.

"Yes. Gold. That is all America can offer. More. Never better. That is all it knows. More, and more, but never that which makes a civilization wonderful."

"It gave me to Sinanju, Little Father."

"I gave you to Sinanju," said Chiun.

In that point, Chiun was largely correct. They had both given Remo to Sinanju, but to admit to truths in an argument was like fighting while holding one's breath. One lost all power. So Remo ignored the remark, and went out to get the rice, and when he returned he found Harold W. Smith was waiting for him with Chiun.

"I could have sworn I got it right down in Cuba," said Remo.

"No problem there," said Smith. He sat on a couch in the small living room as Remo prepared the rice in the open kitchen near the entrance of the apartment. The doors were shut, but Remo knew that Smith carried enough modern sophisticated electronics to tell them if anyone were listening in. As Remo once said, Smith could probably tell if someone were thinking of listening in. Chiun remained in a lotus position, his long fingernails delicately resting on his lap, his back straight, his body at one with itself, so that he looked more in place in the air-conditioned living room than any of the furniture.

"Koreans are very good with electronics," said Chiun. "I trained him."

Remo ignored the remark.

"We have a strange situation developing in Oklahoma. Well, actually throughout America," said Smith. "A band of Ojupa Indians has gone on the warpath."

"I believe they're outnumbered," said Remo. "You do have an army."

"Army," scoffed Chiun. "An army is a collection of human faults and poor discipline multiplied by thousands."

"An army would be useless in this situation," said Smith.

"Aha," said Chiun. "If but your wisdom could be transferred to Remo."

"The President doesn't want to see Americans killing Americans," said Smith.

"Then he should stay out of our cities," said Remo.

Chiun remarked in Korean how true that was, but

cautioned Remo against speaking honestly to Smith, who, because he paid the tribute to Sinanju, Chiun insisted on calling "Emperor Smith."

The saying from the eightieth scroll of the fifth Masterhood of Gi the Major, taken in commentary from Gi the Minor, was:

"Honesty to an emperor from his assassin is like holding the sword by the blade instead of the handle. It can only hurt the assassin."

Remo answered in Korean that he knew that passage, and that speaking honestly to Smith made working easier, not harder.

Chiun answered that what might appear easier was always harder in the long run.

Smith sat in the chilled living room of the resort villa with his briefcase on his lap, listening to Remo and Chiun babble on in Korean as though he weren't there. Voices rose and Smith realized that he was hearing an argument.

He tried to interrupt, and both Chiun and Remo told him to wait a minute. When Remo and Chiun finally turned their heads away from each other in disgust, Smith said:

"We have a problem. This little band of Indians has first defeated the sheriff's office, then the state police, and now the Oklahoma National Guard."

"The Oklahoma National Guard is kind of the army, Little Father," Remo explained.

"What would one expect from an army but to lose a battle?" said Chiun. "After all, Ferris wheels never lose battles."

"They would if they were made in Korea," said Remo.

"Don't argue in front of the emperor," said Chiun, resorting to Korean.

"I'm not arguing," said Remo in English.

"I think you are, Remo," said Smith.

"When I want your opinion I'll ask for it, Smitty. This is personal."

"How can you speak to a fool of an emperor like that?" asked Chiun in Korean. "You're a bigger fool. You're acting white. Whatever crosses your mind comes out your lips."

"It's called honesty, Little Father," said Remo in English.

"It's awfully confusing to hear only one side of an argument," said Smith.

"The confusion is ours, O gracious Emperor, that we should bring any unpleasantness before you who are serenity in yourself."

"Well, thank you. I certainly wouldn't want to get involved in anything personal between you two. But we have a problem. The Indian band has become an army. It has moved all the way up into the Dakotas and now is camped at the Little Big Horn, the site of the great Indian victory over George Armstrong Custer."

"The massacre," said Remo.

"Armies always massacre. Do you think they could assassinate?" asked Chiun, vindicated. "It takes an assassin to assassinate."

"Precisely," said Smith. "Therefore we'd like this army to be immobilized by the removal of its leader, who obviously is the guiding force behind this. It's like an army out of nowhere, a powerful, well-trained army with a spirit for battle rarely seen nowadays."

"You have decided well, O Emperor Smith. For a kingdom with a good assassin needs a small army, and a kingdom with great assassins may need no army at all."

At this point Chiun suggested that perhaps the new tribute for Sinanju should be based on a percentage of America's defense budget. He had heard it was over one trillion a year, and that was outrageous when one considered that for, say, four hundred billion dollars a year, a mere four hundred billion, Smith could be talking about a serious and major upgrade of assassin services—not that Smith and America weren't getting the absolute best as it was now.

"He's not going to shell out four hundred billion dollars, Little Father; besides, what would you do with it?"

"Replace the empty coffers that so disgrace my Masterhood. No other Master of Sinanju has lost so much as a copper coin, while I, because of my negligence with my pupil, because I have taken it upon myself to bring a white into the House of Sinanju, now am left like a pauper with bare treasury."

"Hey, stop this 'white' stuff. I know how the treasure was lost. The North Korean intelligence agency tried to trick you into killing for it, and stole the treasure so they could feed it back to you as though they were discovering a trail from a thief. I know what happened. It was Koreans, not whites, who stole it."

"A single misguided fool. One rotten apple does not a barrel make."

"He killed himself so you'd never find it. Talk of rotten," said Remo. They were both talking in Korean now and Smith threw up his hands and asked them to excuse him. The last words he heard were in English, with Chiun promising to take apart the Indian army in a way that would glorify Smith, and Remo promising that the leaders would be out of the way in no time.

Which was what Smith had come for.

* * *

Miles and miles of trucks and guns waited outside the Little Big Horn for the attack to begin. Only this time it was the American army that had the Indians surrounded instead of vice versa, and General William Tecumseh Buel waited for his orders from Washington.

It was ironic, he thought, that at this new battle of the Little Big Horn there would be no horses. His father was an old cavalryman—though even in his father's time cavalry had meant tanks, not horses—and his grandfather and great-grandfathers were also. In fact, the first Buel to ride in blue for the USA was killed at the Little Big Horn. And while General Buel publicly affirmed he wished no injury to the innocents, in his heart he could not help thinking: Now we even the score.

He set up his heavy artillery behind his half-tracks, which were behind his tanks. The tanks would lead. The infantry would follow. And if the Ojupa wanted to fight it out, well then, there was nothing he could do about it. They would fight. And they would die. Just the night before he had left two roads open so that young Indians, anticipating the glory of finally defeating the white armies, could join the Ojupa.

He had heard their drums and chants all night. He had heard rumors that they had a great new force with them, that finally the great spirits were with them and they could crush the white man once and for all.

"It is a shame that members of our society can feel so alienated as to express such sentiments," General Buel had said publicly. Privately he planned to grind the bastards into Dakota mud under the treads of his Pattons. He was only sorry that he probably would not be able to let the artillery mangle them for long.

He would attack at dawn, approach in five col-

umns, and where they would meet would be the last
live Indian. General Buel would finish him off personally. Maybe a shot to the belly and watch him
squirm, probably the way his own ancestor had
squirmed.

He would then recommend people for medals and
make a wonderful speech about how horrible war
was, perhaps adding the sentiment that from this
horrible battle all mankind might learn to live well
together.

That night he did not sleep. Just before all the
columns began moving, he got a direct call from the
President.

"Bill," said the President, "I've got good news for
you."

"What?" asked General Buel warily.

"I think we can stop this thing without bloodshed."

"Good," said General Buel, his voice cracking. "How
are we going to do that?"

"Just hold your fire and wait for the results. I've
got it covered."

"May I know how, sir?" asked General Buel.

"No," said the President.

"As you say, sir," said General Buel. "But those
Indians seem pretty hostile. I'd hate to have to be on
the defensive in this case, Mr. President, sir."

"I guarantee that everything will be taken care of,"
said the President.

"And if it isn't?"

"Ah, but it always is," said the President.

"Perhaps I can give some assistance."

"They don't need help. It's all taken care of."

"Very good," General Buel said, and hung up
laughing. He knew the last crew who had tried to
enter the tight Indian bivouac ended up tied to a
tree with their throats cut. He would give the Presi-

dent until noon and then open fire. A battle at high noon, he thought.

It would be like an inferno in these Dakota hills. The sun would be directly overhead, and fighting men always consumed more water anyhow. He would drive them away from the riverbank. He would get them into a small valley without water, then let them suffer under the sun as his great-grandfather must have done in these very hills, many years ago.

3

It was a long way from Oklahoma to the Dakotas, but as the stranger said:

"It's always a long way into courage."

He always made so much sense just when someone was ready to call the whole thing off. After all, how could a small band of Indians beat the United States government today, when the odds were even worse than a hundred years ago? But he pointed out that the odds were never good at the beginning of a victory, only at the end.

An engineering student from a college in Iowa pointed out this was absolute nonsense. He was a Plains Indian who had felt overwhelmed by his studies and just enlisted in the cause to get away. He was willing to fight alongside his brothers, but he wasn't going to believe nonsense.

"Look around you. That's the real U.S. Army out there. They got tanks miles deep, and behind them infantry, and behind them artillery. We're not trapping them like a hundred years ago. They're trapping us."

"We beat 'em before," said one brave.

"Custer was outnumbered. We had the numbers then. Now they got 'em."

And some of the young men, who had been thinking there would be only victories and glory, suddenly
had second thoughts.

"I thought they always outnumbered us, but we
beat 'em because we were braver, cleaner, closer to
the earth. But finally their numbers prevailed."

"We outnumbered them at the Little Big Horn.
Custer was the one showing foolhardy bravery. That's
why he died and we didn't."

The revelation threatened to send panic through
the new Indian army, but as always the stranger
seemed to be able to turn things around.

He pointed out that the Israelis were almost always outnumbered, but they won regularly. The engineering student commented that they were better
trained. How much training did this new army have?

"It has the training of its fathers. It has the right-
ness of its cause. Others may want to spend time
playing with guns, but the Indian nation has wasted
too much time already. You wouldn't be living in
reservations today if you hadn't waited too long.
What do you have to lose? The white man's pickup
trucks? The white man's whiskey, which makes you
crazy? You have nothing to lose but your shame."

The stranger in the suit was brilliant, better even
than back in Oklahoma, Little Elk and Running Deere
had to admit. He could take anyone and make him
want to run straight into the guns.

They had decided by now that the stranger had to
be an Indian spirit come back to help them in their
struggle. After all, he did appear in the sacred fire,
and the sacred fire went out when he arrived. He
did come with the chanting of the medicine man. He
did seem to have some very special powers. He never
tired, and he knew who everyone was.

The question was, which Indian spirit? And the

answer was to ask the medicine man, if they could find him. But somehow the stranger found out about their concerns and got them aside just before the big battle with the federal troops, even as the sun was breaking over the Dakota plains, even as the tanks over the hills made the ground tremble and half-tracks created dust storms that looked like the end of the world.

"Look," he said, his face almost shining with joy. "What are you guys worried about? Do you care who I am? Would it help to know who I am? I've got my needs and loves just like the rest of you. I'm a lot like all of you. Maybe with you guys I've found a place I haven't had for a long time. Whatever it is, know this, above all: I am with you in your war."

"Do you have a name?" asked Little Elk. He had a clipboard in his hand. He was going to let the first waves of tanks go through into the center, and then break out along a U.S. highway and try to circle back on the rear of the federal columns. The stranger had thought it was a brilliant plan. Little Elk was discovering, as the stranger predicted, that he was, after all, a military genius. If so many people didn't get killed in wars, he would like to fight one a week.

"What name would you like?"

"You have more than one?" asked Running Deere.

"Sure, but lately I haven't had one. I think you great guys ought to have your own name for me. Your special name."

"We asked your name. This isn't playtime," snapped Little Elk. He had become a brusque, efficient leader in the last few weeks, and he didn't like to waste time anymore. Losing time was like losing life itself, especially when a major battle was about to begin.

"Arieson," said the stranger. "Call me Mr. Arieson. And I'm an old friend of the Ojupa."

"Well, we certainly need you now," said Little Elk, going back to his command post, back to his new platoon leaders, back to all the braves who looked to him now that their hour of destiny was near. He loved it.

Chiun was worse than ever. It was more than the complaining. Remo had never seen him attack furniture and machines before. While packing, he broke the washer-dryer that came with the villa in Flora del Mar. He said he was not a washerwoman. He shredded the air conditioner. He sent the television flying five times, until he finally ended up throwing the pieces into the steamy canal outside their stucco abode.

It took fifteen golf carts to carry Chiun's steamer trunks to the airport limousine. The resort's registration desk had lost their account and thought they could make Chiun wait.

He just walked out. They made the mistake of sending a manager after him. Chiun kept the manager.

"You can't keep someone. It's called slavery," said Remo. "I'll carry the trunks."

"I didn't give you Sinanju so you could be a slave," said Chiun.

"You've got to give back the manager. He's not yours. It's stealing."

"They sent him. He's mine."

"What's wrong?"

"Have you read the histories of Sinanju? Have you examined the stars? Don't you know what's wrong?"

"No," said Remo.

"Then read our histories. At least you didn't let them get stolen."

And then, in South Dakota, at the airport, Chiun seemed to go too far, even for Chiun. He refused to leave the parking lot, refused to let any cars move by him, and looked around, ready to take on the world.

"There. Even here in this backward part of America they desecrate your parking lots with those signs. You are a decrepit culture. And you're going to get worse."

Chiun's long fingernail pointed down to a painting of a wheelchair in the parking lot. The sign showed the space was reserved for the handicapped.

"What's wrong with that?" asked Remo. Even as they were landing, Remo had seen the army forces massing for miles down the roads leading to the Little Big Horn. It was a war he intended to stop. And if he wanted to succeed he didn't have much time to waste in parking lots.

"These are the best spots. They are closest to everything. And they are reserved for the wrong people. They should be given to your best people, your prize athletes, perhaps even to your assassins if your culture had advanced far enough to start producing them."

"Handicapped people are not our worst people. They're people who have been denied certain physical abilities, and as a decent country, unlike some vicious Oriental ones, we take care of them better. If they have a hard time walking, we give them the shortest route. I like it. It's one of the sanest things we've ever done."

"Ruination," said Chiun. He was not moving.

"What's wrong?"

"You do not see it?"

"No. C'mon."

"Your whole country is doomed."

"You always said it wasn't worth saving anyhow. Let's go."

"And this doesn't bother you?" said Chiun, smiling wanly and shaking his head.

"No. I said so. Let's go."

"I'll explain then," said Chiun. "Many of these people who are in wheelchairs have been injured because perhaps at a moment of crisis their minds wandered. Maybe they thought of something else while they drove their cars and did not have time to avoid an accident. You are rewarding lack of excellence. And in so doing you are promoting lack of concentration in your populace."

"Chiun," said Remo, "a lot of people suffered accidents that weren't their fault, and a lot of people were born with problems, so let's go."

"There is no such thing as an accident. There are events you have failed to control."

"Chiun, will you tell me what's wrong?"

"Read your histories."

"I'll read the histories. Let's go."

"You promise now because you want to get on to another silly little assignment."

"What's wrong?"

"Armies. I hate armies."

"You loved the assignment back in Flora del Mar."

"I would like anything that would get us out of that dump," said Chiun.

"It was a nice resort. Let's go."

"An army," said Chiun, "steals the bread out of the mouth of an assassin. An army—"

"I know, Little Father. I read the histories of Sinanju," said Remo, and to get him moving repeated that armies terrorized populations, promoted amateurism, instability, and loss of wealth to a host nation, and worse, gave a monarch the idea that perhaps an assassin wasn't necessary. A monarch often thought, wrongly, if he could have a hundred thousand killers for a pittance each, why would he need one assassin who would cost a fortune? There were many examples in the histories of Sinanju of a Master having to show a monarch his army was useless before he could get hired.

And as they drove a rented car toward Little Big Horn National Park, Chiun repeated the examples, with exactly what tribute was given, and at the end of each account he would mention that that tribute too was lost when Remo was off doing other things while Chiun was hot on the trail of the thief.

"We're never going to find that treasure, so stop carping about what you can't do anything about, and let's get on with this assignment."

"I can do something about it," said Chiun.

"Good. Let me know so I can help."

"You can never help."

"Then what is it you're doing?"

"I'm reminding you," said Chiun, nodding in sour satisfaction.

The entire national park was sealed off by military police. No one could enter without a pass. No civilians could stay on the road.

"All civilians should evacuate to the nearest area designated safe, sir," said the MP, his white helmet glistening in the sun, his sidearm polished in its holster, his boots immaculate.

"Thanks," said Remo, gliding past him. He wore his usual dark T-shirt and gray slacks. Chiun had on his gray traveling kimono and refused to wear the black kimono with red trim indicating a Sinanju Master was performing work. He did not think armies should ever be considered work.

The MP issued the threat again.

"Civilians are not allowed in the designated combat zone," he said.

Remo grabbed his brass belt buckle in two fingers and yanked the MP after them to a nearby jeep. Another MP ran up to help, his sidearm drawn. Chiun got him with his fingernails, and pressing nerves in the MP's neck, convinced him that driving them both into the combat zone was in their best interest.

Thus did they pass the miles and miles of cannon, tanks, and half-tracks, with Chiun complaining constantly.

"When I think of the billions your country spends on its armies, every tank costing many millions, every artillery shell costing five thousand dollars apiece, I am appalled at what a mere four hundred billion dollars would do in tribute to Sinanju."

"What would it do? Sit there?"

"The treasures are living things. They span all ages."

"They sit there," said Remo, and Chiun refused to answer such a low and base insult. Of course, he could have said he was planning to move them to a bigger building to show the glories of Sinanju to the rest of the world. But Remo knew that almost every Master for the last twenty-five centuries had planned to do that and never gotten anywhere, so Chiun could not dispute Remo's charge. Instead, he chose to sit in wounded silence.

As they approached the perimeter of the army encampment they heard groans. The morning attack had been called off. Some of these young volunteers complained that they might never get a chance to fire their weapons in combat.

"Armies," scoffed Chiun. "Soldiers."

"I was once a marine," said Remo.

"And that's why it took so much more time for me to break you of so many absolutely bad habits. You used to think enduring pain was a virtue, not the stupidity of ignoring the wisdom of your body talking to you."

Several soldiers, their M-16's cradled in their arms and the dust of the day on their khaki uniforms, their eyes blackened so they could see better in the glare of the sun, warned the two not to proceed farther.

"There are hostiles up there," said one freckle-faced lad with a bayonet stuck in his belt.

"I'm with one," said Remo.

"He an Indian?" asked the young soldier.

Remo saw Chiun thinking of explaining the difference to the young man between the heavenly perfect people and others, like Africans, Indians, and whites. Chiun could be physical in his lessons at times.

"We don't have time, Little Father," he said.

So instead, Chiun simply endured another injustice from the ungrateful society he served and followed Remo along the little valley. Up ahead they could sense the river. There was a way the earth responded to its water. Some people using divining rods could, crudely, sense the water too. But Remo and Chiun just knew the water was there, and they also knew there was a large encampment of people.

A young man with dark hair and high cheekbones, and a hunting rifle with a big bore, fidgeted inside a foxhole and then chose to rise from it as though trying to surprise Remo and Chiun.

"White man, your time has come," he said, and Remo just walked over him, pushing him back down into the hole. No talk was needed.

They both knew what they were looking for and they both knew how to find a command headquarters. It was always the same. Command headquarters might be in different places on different battlefields, but they were always located in the same relationship to the units they controlled. There were always subordinates running to and fro, from the low in rank to those not-quite-so-low, and from the not-quite-so-low to those higher up.

One only had to find someone giving an order and ask him who gave him his orders. Then it was easy to follow the chain of running messengers to the head man.

That was it.

All armies were the same.

This was the wisdom of the lessons of Sinanju. The difference between sides was only in the imagination of those sides.

When Remo had first learned this, he became angry. He had fought in Vietnam in the early days as a marine, and said he certainly wasn't like the Vietcong.

"If we're all alike, how come one side wins and one side loses?"

"Because some are trained better and some are trained worse. But they are all trained. And they are trained the same way. Not to think. Not to feel. Not to be. Only to act in some crude way that will make them more effective. An army, Remo, is a mob with its mind taken away."

"A mob doesn't have a mind."

"It most certainly does," answered Chiun. "That is why it runs around in hysteria, blindly attacking anything in front of it. What a mob does not have is control. But it does have a mind."

"So why am I learning this? When am I ever going to need this? I'm in training to fight criminals, not soldiers."

"And I am teaching you Sinanju. Let your silly courts decide who is a criminal and who is not. I am teaching you reality. You will learn armies, because that is the way Sinanju teaches. It teaches thought first, then the body."

So Remo had learned about armies, and dynasties, and how one approached a pharaoh, even though there hadn't been a pharaoh around for over three thousand years and there was little likelihood there would ever be one again. He learned Sinanju, and some of it he learned better than the rest of it.

What he forgot quickly and became bored with was the legends of the Masters, which, as any American over thirteen would recognize, was promotional material for the oldest house of assassins in the world.

And Chiun never stopped tiring of telling him that if he did not learn Sinanju whole he did not know Sinanju. And this meant reverence for the lost treasures as well as the histories. But this admonition was useless after Remo had made the last passage and become himself a Master of Sinanju.

For Chiun it meant he could no longer threaten Remo by telling him that if he did not do something, he would never become a Master.

Because now he was. And thus on that hot summer day, Remo and Chiun, two Masters of Sinanju, walked along the prairieland toward the Little Big Horn, ready to stop the second battle there between the U.S. Army and American Indians.

And no one noticed that the two men strolling along under the sun did not sweat, nor did they kick up dust under their feet. And no one noticed that they seemed remarkably unaffected by warnings from braves with guns.

They did not notice these things until it was too late to notice, and then they noticed nothing. A platoon of machine-gunners from an eastern tribe lay forever in the land that once belonged to the

Sioux. Cannoneers from Minnesota reservations lay draped over the barrels of the guns they had learned to use only that morning.

Right up the organization created by the military genius of Little Elk moved Remo and Chiun, until they found a long flatbed truck with many antennae sticking out of it, and several men squatting over maps nearby. Only one was out of uniform. He wore a suit and tie and carried a briefcase, and every once in a while the men in the new Ojupa uniform, deerskins, would turn to him with a question. And he would answer it.

They called him Mr. Arieson.

"That's our man," said Remo. There were only a few guards protecting the command group. But even if there were many, it wouldn't matter.

It would not be too hard to move in, take out the leader, perhaps keep the subordinates for a while in some safe place like a locked truck or one of the manned vehicles preparing for this war, and let the army disintegrate into an aimless mob.

Then the remnants could be handled by social workers and sheriffs.

Remo ambled toward the group whistling a tune from a Walt Disney film he liked, the words to which he remembered only randomly, but it was a cheery little thing about going off to work.

He noticed Chiun was not with him, and assumed this was because of Chiun's distaste for fighting soldiers. But then he heard Chiun's voice calling after him, saying what Remo had never heard before.

"It won't work. Come back. Let us return to Sinanju. The time to wait is at hand. Let the world go crazy."

"What're you talking about?" laughed Remo.

"You won't be able to do what you want," said Chiun. Remo did not even turn around.

"See you when I'm done."

"You won't be," said Chiun.

Remo whistled ". . . it's off to work we go" as the first guards threw up their hands, warning him to halt, and lowered the automatic weapons as a sign of what would happen to him if he didn't.

He spun them backward, sweeping his palms upward, bowling them into the dust, and walking on. He took a bayonet charge and kept moving. The last two guards protecting headquarters got off a few shots, and Remo slapped their guns away from them, catching the weapons as they fell and never breaking stride until he walked into the command council of the new Indian army, headed by the men now known as the fearless Ojupa.

He dropped the guns on the map. That gave the kneeling men something to do. Then he went for the man with the thick neck in the three-piece suit. Remo noticed there was no perspiration on the man's forehead, although he was out in the sun.

Was that what Chiun meant by his work being useless, that he had spotted something in this man that showed he knew Sinanju?

But why wouldn't Remo spot it?

Remo did not lunge with a simple stroke. He approached as though offering his own body as a target, but in reality he wanted to make the man commit to a thrust so Remo would see how he moved.

But the man didn't move. He didn't even exhale properly. His eyes seemed to burn, and he was laughing.

To Little Elk and Running Deere and the rest of the commanders of the new Indian army, it looked like some weirdo had startled them by throwing guns on their maps and then walked over to Mr. Arieson and leaned backward.

They looked up to see how he had gotten through their defenses. Where were their guards? A quick glance at the strewn bodies on the dusty grasslands told them.

Running Deere, now always ready for action, always ready to charge, took his own sidearm and got off a shot to the stranger's head. Apparently the weapon misfired, because while there was noise and smoke, the bullet didn't strike anything. He fired again. And missed again.

The stranger moved as though segments of time disappeared. Now he was leaning backward and now he was between Running Deere and Mr. Arieson. And before he could think, Running Deere got off two more rounds. And they missed the stranger and they missed Mr. Arieson.

Only Remo and Mr. Arieson knew they hadn't missed. Remo had lured the shot to see what effect a bullet would have on the man who did not sweat or move in to deliver a sucker punch. The sidearm was a big, slow weapon. There was the pulling of the trigger, the aim of the barrel, the explosion, Remo dropping beneath the line of the bullet and then watching it go past. Both of the bullets landed in a hillock three-quarters of a mile away, shattering a rock. Both of them went through the third button of the vest of Mr. Arieson.

Mr. Arieson had not even bothered to dodge.

He did not wear armor plating. And he was not affected by missiles. Remo fanned the ground, first with little motions of his flat palm against the dry dust, then faster, feeling the air as hard as wood paddles, compressing it with a swooshing sound until in brown fury the dust exploded into a dry storm.

Grass was blown out of the dirt. And still Mr. Arieson did not move.

Running Deere went at the stranger with his hands.
Running Deere kept going, but Remo kept the hands.

"I think I know who you are," said Mr. Arieson,
"but you're white. I've never seen moves like that
from a white man."

"Who are you?"

"I believe I am your enemy," said Mr. Arieson.

Just on the chance that it might work, having tried
several things that didn't, Remo threw a stiff finger
into the right eye of Mr. Arieson.

And this time the dust came back at him in the
form of smoke, like a campfire with strange, sweet
smells.

And Mr. Arieson was gone.

So it had worked. *What* had worked, Remo was not
sure. But something had worked. Mr. Arieson, the
leader of this army, was gone. And now Remo could
turn to the rest of the command.

"Well, fellas, who's for dying today?"

Little Elk went for one of the guns Remo had
dropped on the map. Remo snapped it between his
fingers like a twig.

Three of the other leaders went for their weapons,
but Little Elk, always one step ahead of everyone
else, ordered them to stop.

"It's over," he said. "Mr. Arieson is gone."

And then from nowhere, from the dust and from
the lingering sweet-smelling smoke, came Mr. Arieson's voice. And it was laughing.

"Only the dead have seen the last of me," he said.

On that day, Running Deere died from his wounds.
General William Tecumseh Buel lost his chance to
fight the second battle of the Little Big Horn, and
Remo Williams notified Harold W. Smith, head of
CURE, that after more than two decades, he was
quitting the organization.

"Why? Where are you going? What are you going to do? Has something happened?"

"Yeah. Something has happened," said Remo. "Something bad."

"What?"

"I finally discovered that I'm useless. I've got to do something first."

"What?"

"I'm not sure. But I met something today that I should have known. I'm helpless. For the first time since training, I am absolutely helpless."

"But you put down the revolt."

"I've got a mystery here, little Smitty, and until I unravel it I won't be any good to you, myself, or anyone else."

"The mystery is what you're talking about."

"It wouldn't do any good to explain it, Smitty."

"Why not?" asked Smith.

"Because you're not from Sinanju and you've never read the scrolls."

"Where are you going?"

"To Sinanju."

"Why?"

"Because Chiun is there."

"Has he quit?"

"I think so. And so have I. So long, Smitty."

The line went out in the secured offices of Harold W. Smith, in the gigantic cover installation known as Folcroft Sanitarium on Long Island Sound.

Quitting? thought Smith. So that's what Chiun's message was about. The way Chiun had explained it, it sounded like he was going to give an even greater service to Smith, but was just taking some time to improve himself.

But hearing from Remo, Smith now understood that the flowery tributes to Smith's wisdom and genius, the promise of a return with stronger and better service, were really Chiun's way of saying good-bye.

What was frightening now was not any Indian rebellion, but the great question of how it could get started so easily, and why the normal protective measures of society seemed so pathetically useless.

The United States Army report was alarming. The Ojupa were just a simple group of men who, in a flash, turned into one of the great little armies of mankind, with a fighting spirit rarely seen on earth.

They had developed tactics on the spot that could rival Hannibal or Napoleon. They showed a fighting élan that the finest troops would envy.

But army analysts could not discover why this seemingly normal group of men could become so good, so quickly. The conclusion of this report was that if the same sort of situation turned up elsewhere in the world, neither the U.S. Army nor any other army could handle it. The report also went to the President of the United States, who told his Secretary of Defense not to worry because he had something special that could take care of it like it did at Little Big Horn.

He didn't know he not only didn't have those services, but the world was going to see those same tactics again very soon. Only the dead had seen the last of Mr. Arieson.

4

General Mohammed Moomas, first Democratic People's Leader for Life, inventor of People's Democratic Islamic Revolutionary Social Justice—by which the nation Idra sought not only to live the perfect social and religious life but also to bring compassion, love, and justice to the rest of the world—had a problem.

General Moomas always had a problem. His tiny North African country floating on a sea of oil had spent over forty-two billion dollars fighting imperialism, Zionism, capitalist oppression, atheism, and man's general inhumanity to man, and all he had to show for it were thirteen thousand random murders, a half-dozen plane hijackings, four poisonings, fifty-seven kidnappings, twelve hundred tortures, and the unflagging support of several American columnists, especially when America tried to do something about it.

General Moomas had operated freely for years, financing any revolutionary group willing to throw a hand grenade into a hospital and then claim a victory for social justice. There were always comrade citizens unwilling to accept the total freedom, total joy, total growth and liberty of the Islamic Democratic People's Socialist Revolutionary Nation of Idra.

This was understandable. Satan, Zionism, imperialism, capitalism, and oppression could reach the hearts of the innocent and foolish, and the General had to face the evil. But given a chance, and with the help of whips, chains, electric shocks, and the old-fashioned holy sword cutting pieces off their persons, many people renounced their evil ways.

The truly obstinate, of course, had to be killed. Thus no one spoke a word of unhappiness in General Mohammed Moomas' country.

All this changed when American bombers flew in low over the Mediterranean, outflew the General's latest Soviet planes, penetrated his latest Soviet missiles, and nearly destroyed his home.

For the first time, the people of Idra learned they might have to pay for their leadership in the revolutionary world. Someone out there was shooting back, and shooting at them.

Several colonels debated overthrowing the General. After all, oil prices were falling, and like so many third-world nations, they produced nothing else of benefit to anyone else on the planet. There was no industry in Idra. There was a steel mill once. They had brought it from Czechoslovakia. The steel would build homes and hospitals, tanks and guns. But when the Czechs left, it just rusted away, like all the weapons the Idrans bought from outside.

Thus, while there were demonstrations in London and Europe over the American bombing, and while several American columnists were screaming daily that bombing Idra did no good—it could not stop terrorism, they said—the General was almost overthrown.

A group of colonels stormed to his desert sanc-

tuary. They all drove in their Mercedes-Benz se-
dans. There were fifteen thousand colonels in the
Idra Islamic Revolutionary Socialist Defense Forces,
roughly a third of all the military. The rest were
mostly generals. But if one was a general he didn't
have to leave his French-built air-conditioned home.
Therefore the colonels did all the dirty work, like
driving out to the desert to discuss the basic issue of
Idra—what had they gotten for their oil money but
American bombs?

General Moomas, a handsome man with curly hair
and dark penetrating eyes, had not become a revolutionary leader without being able to handle a mob.
He invited the entire fifteen thousand colonels to a
traditional bedouin feast of lamb, so that from his
hand to their mouths would only be sustenance.

General Moomas knew he could provide this traditional feast. A ship from New Zealand had docked
just three weeks before and that meant plenty of
lamb. Considering Korean stevedores had just arrived to offload, and an army of French cooks had
just signed on for the Idra marines, and Italian me-
chanics were always on hand for the trucks, this
traditional feast was now possible.

In years past, Idra women could outcook an army
of Paris chefs, using only the meager fare of the Idra
desert. But their skills had been lost during modern-
ization, when they were assigned to learn computers
and physics and all the things the Idra men found to
be beyond them and assigned elsewhere to another
gender. Since there was only one other gender in
Idra, cooking fell, like all the dirty work for thousands of years, on the women, some of whom actually did become proficient in those subjects and
promptly left for London, where they could find

work other than posing for news cameras to show how modern Idra was.

Now, as the fragrant aroma of lamb roasting in a thousand imported ovens filled the cold night desert air, General Moomas confronted his brethren to offer an accounting of where all the billions had gone.

"I know I promised you the best air defense money could buy, and look now, American navy air has penetrated those defenses. But I ask you, who would have thought the Russians would flee their posts in our hour of need?"

"I would," said one colonel.

"Then would you have operated the missiles?" asked the General.

There was silence in the desert. Only the mutterings of the French cooks preparing the traditional sweet desserts could be heard.

The desserts were never as good as their wives and mothers used to make, but the French came as close to Idran cooking as Moroccans or Syrians.

Another colonel rose, and this one held a submachine gun. He did not blanch at the guards who outnumbered him and obviously had him in their sights.

"I am a Moslem," he said. "I obey. I obey the teachings of the Koran. I believe there is but one God, and Mohammed is his prophet. I do not believe in killing innocents. I do believe in fighting evil and I do not consider a bomb in a car that will kill any passerby a heroic act of virtue. I thought throwing a man in a wheelchair off a ship was cowardly and disgraceful. If that helps the Palestinian cause, to hell with the Palestinian cause."

There was grumbling like a low volcano from the fifteen thousand that night. Fingers on the triggers of guns aimed at his head closed ever so slightly. If the General hiccuped, the colonel would be dead.

General Moomas raised a hand to silence his officers.

"What is bad about killing a crippled Jew who was a Zionist anyway because he was headed for Israel? It is no crime to kill Zionists."

"It is a dishonor to kill the defenseless," said the colonel.

And here the General laughed. He ordered his aides to bring him American newspapers, and taking one from Washington and one from Boston, read the words of columnists who, every time a pregnant woman was put on board a plane with a bomb to blow herself and the passengers out of the sky, every time a crippled man was thrown off a liner along with his wheelchair, every time someone set off a bomb in a nightclub, or hospital, or nursery in honor of the Palestinian cause, these columnists blamed Israel.

"Only when the root cause of terrorism is erased will terrorism end, and the root cause is the lack of a Palestinian homeland."

There was applause that night in the desert encampment, but the lone colonel continued to speak out.

"There was killing of innocents and kidnapping of innocents long before there was talk of a Palestinian state. Who here thinks it is really honorable to kill women and children and old men to achieve your ends? I am for obliterating Israel. But not for any Palestinians—for us. They have humiliated us in battle. I say we should humiliate them the same way. Not kill old men in wheelchairs and women pregnant with our babies."

"But in the great universities there are many teaching that we are in the right, that the West is decadent and must be overthrown by revolution," said the General. "We are winning the war of propaganda."

"Which is what? What others think of us?"

"Soon, America will turn against Israel, and without American arms, Israel will be weak, and then we shall destroy the Zionist entity."

"They survived all our armies at their birth. They were weak then."

"And so were we. But when we destroy Israel, we shall ride into Jerusalem in glory."

"Who here believes that?" yelled out the young colonel. "Who here really believes we are going to do that? Who here believes we will even fight another war against Israel? I do not care about Israel. Let it burn in hell. I do not care about the Palestinians, as I know you, my brothers, care not also. What I do care about is us. We were once a proud and great people. Our armies fought with honor. We won great victories. We could show mercy because we were strong. We were a haven for people because we were tolerant of those who followed the Book. What have we become now, killers of old men? We think it is all right because some Americans who hate their own country and their allies think any abomination is acceptable.

"We were great before the Europeans arrived in America. We were great while Europeans were living in stone buildings and butchering each other in little feudal kingdoms. The Arab world was truly the home of great learning, and military courage, and honor that was a beacon of enlightenment, not a torch in every part of the world where Islam is taught. We are an honorable people. Why do we allow ourselves to be known for infamy?"

"The Zionists control the media. They tell lies about us."

"It is not Zionist lies I care about, but the truth. And the truth is that we buy our weapons and we buy the people to operate them, and when trouble comes, the foreigners leave us to the bombs of the enemies. That is what I speak of."

"Can you do better?"

"I most certainly can. The first thing we must do is learn to fight a war. If we can't use a weapon ourselves, we won't have the Chinese or North Koreans or Russians use it for us. We will only fight with what we can use ourselves. We will give up our fancy cars, our fancy expense accounts in European hotels, and we will go back to the desert and become an army. And then we will fight our enemies—honorably. We shall give succor to the weak, mercy to the innocent, and honor to our arms."

"And what if we lose?" asked the General.

"Is death so bitter that you fear it more than losing your souls? Is defeat in honorable battle more shameful than impregnating a woman and using her as a living bomb with your unborn child, and worse, having it all planned by some of your generals? Are the words of the decadent West so appealing in your ears that they can deny you your heritage of tolerance and courage, just because you attack their enemies? Where are the Arabs who beat the Frankish knights? Who ground the Hindu armies into submission? Who turned Egypt from a Christian country to an Islamic one? Where are those who civilized Spain? Where, where, where?"

The General, seeing this colonel was reaching the hearts of his men where not even a new car or fine imported food could venture, understood he was losing. And to lose an argument in Idra meant losing your life.

He knew almost every colonel in the country, and he couldn't quite recognize that one.

The man was bearded, with a thickish neck. He stood quite proud. The General would have followed him himself after that speech, which is why he knew the colonel had to die.

"You speak well. You speak with courage. I am promoting you to general and making you leader of any force you wish to use to attack Israel. You may stab the Zionist snake right in the belly. Your weapons will be waiting for you offshore, or in Haifa, or Tel Aviv, or any Zionist city you care to name. Good luck. Good hunting, take any volunteers you wish. Any of you who wish to go with our new general, feel free. There will be bonuses."

And with that, the General went into his tent. He took his most trusted adviser into conference, and there whispered to him:

"He will not get followers, of course. No one is going to give up his Mercedes to die. They wouldn't give up their Mercedeses for Toyotas, let alone Israeli bullets. When he fails to get followers for the mission, tell him you will join him. Tell him you have a fine house in the capital you wish to give him for his courage. He will not trust you but he cannot turn down your house, after all. When he comes to dinner, poison him."

"Will he not suspect something?"

"Of course he will suspect something. But the beauty of our plan is that a house is too valuable to refuse to look at. He will think he can fool us by convincing us he believes our story, and then try to kill us shortly thereafter when he thinks we think he is fooled. Do you understand, O brother?"

"No one is smarter than you, O brother and leader."

"I am not the leader because grass grows on my forehead." General Moomas smiled.

But suddenly there was cheering from outside. Guns were fired into the air. War shrieks were heard. Columns of men were marching through the scrub and sand of the Idra desert. And to the General's vast relief, they were not marching toward him. They were marching toward the sea. They had left their Mercedeses behind, their lamb dinners served on Royal Doulton china, their almost-Arab desserts. A cry was heard and echoed through the hard night:

"Let us die at the gates of Jerusalem."

The General had often ended speeches like that. He would end them and then go home to his air-conditioned palace, and the cheering mobs would go to their homes, and they would all live another day to hear the same words.

But no one was going home. No one was even bothering to drive his Mercedes.

"They will tire in a half-mile and come back to their cars. Then I will tell them they are the real revolutionary heroes and any fools who continue to march with that colonel, excuse me, general, are not heading for Jerusalem, but death. The real road to Jerusalem is through my leadership."

But no one came back that evening or the next evening. The General heard the colonels had organized themselves into platoons and battalions. They trained without comforts. They marched in the desert heat, and if they did not know how to fix a vehicle, they did not use it. Eventually two things happened. Some vehicles were abandoned but others were made to work. The Idran soldiers even became proficient at tank warfare. They did not bother with revolutionary speeches, but learned their weapons, discovered their new leaders, and prepared to live or die in battle.

Their new leader from the ranks of colonels would not give his name. But one of the colonels, a bit shrewder than the rest, pressed him on several occasions to give his name. After all, if he were going to lead them against Israel, they should at least know what to call him.

"Arieson," he said. "You can call me Arieson."

"That's not an Arab name," said the colonel.

"It most certainly is," said Arieson. "You have been a friend of mine in ages past who would shame the rest of all mankind with your glory."

And the shrewd colonel passed this information to a German reporter in the capital, and that reporter relayed the information to his superiors, and finally the word got to a planning station outside Tel Aviv.

The Arabs were putting together a tough little army the likes of which hadn't been seen in the Middle East since the eighth century, when Arab armies leapt out of the desert to conquer a massive empire in a thunderclap of time.

"How many in that army?" asked Israeli intelligence.

"Fifteen thousand."

"That's nothing."

"You've got to see these guys," they were told. "They're good."

"How good can an Idran be?" asked the Israeli command.

"You'd better not find out."

They dismissed the report. The only time the Idran army had ever fired their weapons in anger was against some defenseless African tribes. And when they heard where the Idrans were going to attack, they were absolutely hysterical. The plan, as they found out, was to launch a drive right into the major base defending the Negev, prove the Israelis could be beaten even though they had larger forces, and then take prisoners and retreat fighting all the way to the Egyptian border.

None of them in the planning room of the Israeli defense forces outside Tel Aviv thought that within a short time they would be desperately calling up reserves from around Jerusalem to help out their armored units trapped in the Negev.

Sinanju, home of the House of Sinanju, glorious House of Sinanju, smelled as it had the last time Remo had visited it. Waste from the pigsties flooded out into the main street, and the sewage system the Masters had brought the villagers lay unused for want of anyone to install it.

The system was made of the finest Carrara marble, with pipes hewn by hand and polished smooth. Unfortunately, that particular sewer system had to be installed by Roman engineers. In the year 300 B.C. travel was not as safe as it was nowadays, and the sewer pipes arrived in Sinanju but the engineers didn't. So the pipes lay unused all about, while the town stank.

Remo commented on this as the two of them arrived on the main road from Pyongyang.

"It's amazing the thieves didn't take the pipes also," said Chiun. "But what did you care? You are not even coming with me for love of Sinanju but to find out how to kill someone you cannot kill."

"Do you want me to tell you I love a pigsty?" asked Remo.

"New Jersey is not a pigsty?" asked Chiun.

"It doesn't smell like Sinanju."

"It doesn't produce Masters of Sinanju either," said Chiun.

At the entrance to the village, the elders lined up to greet the returning Master. They were happier this time, because now they could assure him that no treasure was missing. Of course it wasn't missing because it had already gone the last time Chiun had returned to discover that the head of North Korean intelligence had stolen it in a ruse to get the House of Sinanju to work for Kim Il Sung.

When this had failed and the chief committed suicide, which was wise, he had unfortunately taken with him the secret of the treasure's whereabouts. Since he had not even told his glorious leader, Kim Il Sung, the whereabouts of the treasure, it was lost forever.

That North Korea could not reimburse the House of Sinanju was evident. The only question remained whether Kim Il Sung should be punished for the misdeeds of his subordinate, and the answer was yes. But what punishment might be appropriate, Chiun could not decide right away, and in tribute, Kim Il Sung chose to build three new superhighways to the village and place a full chapter glorifying the House of Sinanju in every textbook in every school in North Korea.

Thus, amid Marxist-Leninist ideology would appear the family-history tree of the Masters of Sinanju, with praises on one hand for worker committees and on the other for pharaohs and kings who paid on time.

That this confusion was not protested was not unusual. The only thing most students knew about Marxist-Leninist dialectics was that they had better pass it.

So hundreds of thousands of students now learned by rote that Akhnaton in his righteousness gave forty Nubian statues of gold to Master Gi, and King Croesus of Lydia did pay in gold four hundred plowduts, and Darius of Persia offered jewels of one hundred obol weight—along with the principle of the invincibility of the masses over oppression.

This satisfied Chiun that Kim Il Sung was doing all he could. Especially when Remo and Chiun were met at the Pyongyang People's Airport by three thousand students waving the flag of the Masters of Sinanju and all singing:

"Praised be thy glorious house of assassins, may thy truth and beauty reign forever in a world glorified by thy presence."

Remo had waited impatiently with Chiun.

"They don't even know what they're singing," he whispered.

"Never disdain a tribute. Your American students should learn such manners."

"I hope they never learn those verses," Remo had said, so naturally, by the time they reached the village, Chiun had collected this major injustice of the trip and happily stored it where he nurtured all the injustices Remo put upon him, so that they could bear fruit that could then be sprinkled upon their daily lives.

"Perhaps you think the village elders of Sinanju are fools too, waiting as they are to pay tribute."

"No," said Remo. "Why shouldn't they pay tribute? We've fed them for four thousand years."

"We are from them," said Chiun.

"I'm not," said Remo.

"Your son will be."

"I don't have a son," said Remo.

"Because you play around with all those Western floozies. Marry a good Korean girl and you will produce an heir and we will train him. He too will

marry Korean, and by and by no one will know there
was a white stain in the Masterhood."

"If that's the case," said Remo, "maybe you already
have a white ancestor. Have you ever thought about
that?"

"Only in my nightmares," said Chiun, alighting
from the car and receiving the deep bows of many
old men.

Remo looked behind them. As far as the eye could
see, four lanes of absolutely unused highway spun
into the Korean hills toward Pyongyang. He knew
there were two other highways coming from the
village, equally unused. Occasionally, he heard, a yak
might wander over one of the massive thoroughfares
and leave a dropping, whereupon a North Korean
helicopter would speed out of Pyongyang with a
brush and a scoop and clean it up, so that Sinanju
Highways One, Two, and Three would remain always immaculate. It was the least they could do in
lieu of the treasure of Sinanju.

"Greetings," said Chiun to the elders. "I have returned with my son, Remo. I do not wish to hold it
against him that he did not help search for the
treasure when it was first discovered missing. After
all, there are many worse to blame, those who did
not offer up their lives to recover it."

There were low nods from the men along Sinanju
Highway One.

"You might wonder why I hold nothing against
Remo," Chiun said.

"No, they don't. I'm sure they don't wonder that,
Little Father," said Remo.

The men looked up, worried. Two Masters were
disagreeing. Either one could wreak punishment on
them that they would wish they had not lived to
endure.

Chiun quieted them with a hand. "He does not mean that. We all know you wish to know why I will not hold this against Remo. First, because he has come home to study. He will read the scrolls of the history of Sinanju now, and why?"

"I know why, Little Father."

"Shhh. They don't know why. He will read the scrolls of the histories of Sinanju because he has come up against something he cannot defeat, and why cannot he defeat this?"

No one answered.

"He cannot defeat this because he does not know what it is," said Chiun.

"I would if you'd tell me," said Remo.

"It would do you no good. You cannot handle this person until you recover the treasure of Sinanju," said Chiun.

"Now I know you're running a game, Little Father," said Remo, who decided not to wait around anymore to hear that. He knew Chiun knew what they were up against, just as he knew Chiun would not tell him right away. But sooner or later he would have to, if for nothing else than to gloat.

Remo was not ready for what he heard as he walked away, though, not ready for the price that was now being offered on his behalf.

"But being regretful and full of great remorse, my son, Remo, knows he must make up for the treasure to all of us, and he has decided to give the village of Sinanju a son."

Heads raised. There was applause.

"From one of the village beauties of Sinanju," said Chiun.

"There is no such thing," said Remo.

"No child, no help with your enemy," said Chiun.

"He's your enemy too, Little Father."

"That he is, but you are the one more anxious to finish him now. Besides, you cannot stay childless all your life, and if you have a son with some white woman, she could run off like all loose white women do and not care for the child. If you have a child with a Sinanju maiden, you know he will be raised honored and glorified because his father is a Master of Sinanju."

"I don't want a child."

"You don't know till you try."

"Just let me at the scrolls," said Remo. "I know if you recognized that guy, the answer has to be in the scrolls. So that's why I'm going to read them again. But marriage, no."

"One night. One moment. One sending of your seed to meet an egg. I do not ask for a lifelong commitment. Let the mother give that."

"Just show me the scrolls."

"No one-night marriage, no scrolls."

"But you used to beg me to read the scrolls."

"That was when you didn't want to read them."

Remo sighed. He looked around. The sooner he got the scrolls, the sooner he would know what Chiun had recognized back at Little Big Horn.

And what would be so bad about one night? He wouldn't have to raise the child. And Sinanju would have an heir to the Masterhood.

Would he want his child to know Sinanju? Funny, he thought, looking down at the wood shacks and the mud walks being serviced by three major empty highways, he could not conceive of having a son without him learning Sinanju, becoming Sinanju, no matter what the cost to him and the boy. It was the way of things.

He just didn't plan on making the mother a woman from this village necessarily. He was still American enough to expect to fall in love before he married someone and made a child.

"All right," he said. So what? he thought. Why not? How bad could one night be?

"Then I shall open all the scrolls again to you. You shall read about the difference between the laudations to the pharaoh of the Upper Nile and the Lower Nile. You shall see how not to be tempted by a Ming courtesan. All the things I tried to teach you before, you will know. And you will marry a good girl, too. I will select her."

"I didn't say you'd choose," said Remo. "I'll choose."

"As you wish. Select the loveliest. Choose the smartest. Do as you will. I do not wish to run your life," said Chiun, beaming.

But when Remo finally met the young women, he learned that all the good-looking ones had used the three main highways to leave Sinanju, and those left were the ones who would not leave their mothers, those who knew that even in Pyongyang, where there were more men than anywhere else in the world, they could still not find someone, and Poo Cayang.

Poo weighed 250 pounds and knew two words in English. They were not "yes" and "no,' they were not "hello, Joe" or even "good-bye, Joe." They were "prenuptial agreement."

Every other word in her vocabulary was Korean, specifically the Sinanju dialect which Remo spoke. But Poo's mother did the negotiating for her.

Poo did not think of herself as overweight but rather as fully blossomed. Poo had not gotten married because so far no one in Sinanju was good enough for her, she felt. And she didn't see any potential in Pyongyang. She was the baker's daughter, and before anyone else in Sinanju got their breads or cakes, Poo chose first. It was to be understood this arrangement was to continue if she were to marry the white Master of Sinanju.

More important and more specific, she was never to be forced to leave Sinanju or be more than an hour's walk from her mother.

"You'd stay here even if I left?" asked Remo.

"Yes," she said.

"Will you marry me?" said Remo.

"We haven't gotten to the ownership of the home yet," said Poo.

"Will it be in Sinanju?"

"It must."

"It's yours," said Remo.

"Now for point eighteen," said Poo. "Pots, pans, dinnerware."

"Yours," said Remo.

5

It was a brilliant plan. Even the Israelis had to admire it after it was pulled off. Under cover of night, thousands of dhows, old Arab fishing boats, set sail from Idra across the Mediterranean for the Israeli coast.

If the Idran army had used the new Soviet destroyers or the French gunboats, or protected the craft with overflights of their fighters flown by Russians, the Israelis would have picked them up, and certainly the U.S. Sixth Fleet, which dominated the Mediterranean, would have seen them on the most advanced radar system in the world.

But the dhows were wood. And they were sailed by Iraqis who knew their craft from the Euphrates. The Iraqis had no love for the Idrans or Syrians, and actually hated the Iranians, who were not Arabs at all but Persians. They were old feuds. But they too had met a Mr. Arieson and, as they told their Idran passengers, there was something about him that made fighting a war so worthwhile.

"We feel good. We feel proud of ourselves," they said.

"So do we," said their passengers as the great fleet of little wooden boats made its way slowly out into the Mediterranean. The stranger even seemed to be able to control the weather, because during the day, when airplanes would normally see something almost a mile across, there was fog. And one night they came upon the great Sixth Fleet, outlined dark against the sky, stretching for miles in its stateliness and awesome power, lights blinking from the great carriers as the finest fighter pilots in the world left the decks to challenge the world.

They could hear the waves against the wooden prows, and many were the men who silently prayed to their desert god that the great U.S. Sixth Fleet would move off into the night to dominate some other stretch of sea.

But to the horror of many, Mr. Arieson ordered the wooden fleet to turn in to the metal monsters from the West. They were not even trying to escape. They were attacking.

"What are you doing, General?" asked the colonel whom Arieson had made his chief of staff. He was from a mountain tribe deep inland in the country now named Idra. He hated the idea of the sea, but through his courage had nailed his body into the boat with a smile on his face to show his men the proper leadership. Now he was overwhelmed by the stupidity of small wooden boats attacking the greatest navy the world had ever seen.

He pulled at Mr. Arieson's sleeve. It felt like stone covered by cloth.

"What are you doing?" he asked again.

"We'll never see a prize like that again."

"Prize?" asked Colonel Hamid Khaidy, who had studied briefly at Russian military schools and learned they thought of the Sixth Fleet as one of the three great threats in the world, the other two being kept secret from non-Russians.

"Just think of the glory in attacking the U.S. Sixth Fleet. The finest sailors in the world, commanded by the finest officers, with the finest pilots, and the latest weapons. This truly is a challenge."

"But isn't it the purpose of war to win? Aren't you supposed to attack where they are weakest?"

"What's the point in that? Who would you beat then? If you want a victory like that, go fight a clinic for the terminally ill."

"I have never read of tactics where you go looking for the biggest fight in the world," said Hamid Khaidy. He had the hard face of a desert warrior and cold night-black eyes.

"Don't worry. You'll love me for it," said Mr. Arieson. He smiled and let out a soft song about great battles, great Arab battles, how they defeated the Crusaders at the Horns of Hattin, and now how they would defeat the great U.S. Sixth Fleet that stretched across the horizon and could bounce signals off the night moon and demolish any city it chose. Arrogant it was, and greater still, a living electronic and metal dragon that ruled this sea where Western culture was born.

"Know this," said Mr. Arieson, "and pass it along. The word 'admiral' is an Arab word. Once you were great sea fighters too. You shall be known as such again."

"We shall die in this landless place," said Khaidy.

"Then die with honor, for surely you will die either way," said Arieson, and guided the little pieces of the vast wooden latticework bobbing on the coal-black sea like little water bugs toward the metal monsters in the distance.

The electronics rooms on the U.S. ships could detect a fly on the wingtip of a missile cruising at Mach 10. They could differentiate between a nuclear warhead half a world away and a normal explosive. They could do this with missiles, planes, and even artillery shells behind inland mountain ranges.

They could listen to telephone conversations and shortwave radios from Rome to Tripoli to Cairo to Tel Aviv.

They knew when propeller aircraft took off from Athens and when a balloon landed on a hilltop in Cyprus.

They could pick up submarines cruising near the sea bottom and tell a manta ray from a shark three miles down. They could identify a torpedo twenty miles away just as it launched its strike run.

But they could not pick up wood on the surface of the ocean.

Wooden sailing boats had disappeared from active combat almost a century before.

The Idran fleet of a thousand tiny boats bobbed into the great Sixth Fleet that night, and when the little boats were close, the fear became the greatest. It was as though a civilization many stories high loomed above them, churning along with propellers that made great gurgling hisses all about the flimsy wooden boats.

"What do we do now?" asked Khaidy in a whisper. He felt as though they could be sucked under by the great propellers of the aircraft carriers and would no more be noticed than a toothpick going under in a sink.

"We attack for the glory of your tribes and your nation and your faith," cried out Mr. Arieson, and Khaidy prayed for help from his desert god.

But Mr. Arieson was prepared. From boat to boat the order was issued.

"Unwrap the green bundles."

Khaidy had remembered that the bundles were

too heavy to be food and too solid to be ammunition. He did not know why Mr. Arieson had some placed on board each dhow in the center, beneath the ammunition.

Now, as one was unwrapped, he saw a nearby gun get pulled to it and stick there. They were magnets. Magnets with ropes. They were magnet ladders, and now Khaidy, always quick of mind, understood what they would be used for. The Idran army was going to board some of the American ships.

And why not? The boats were actually safest here under the ships, because they were in the one place the big guns, the rockets and the airplanes could not reach. Mr. Arieson had showed them how to defeat the finest and most modern navy of all time. Up the ladders went the men of Idra, knives in their teeth, glory in their hearts, and when they hit the decks of the USS *James K. Polk*, they let out a battle cry and attacked.

The captain of the *Polk*, scanning reports of air activity over the Crimea, heard the yell and thought it was some kind of party. The captain commanding the marine contingent called out his men, who put up a good fight but were outnumbered. The air pilots had never been that well trained in hand-to-hand combat, under the assumption that if they had to fight someone with their hands, they were already rendered useless for flying. The sailors fought with mops and brooms. But it was no use.

Up went the green banner of Islam aboard the USS *Polk* with its nuclear weapons and aircraft, and for the first time since the Battle of Lepanto centuries before, the Mediterranean had a credible Arab naval presence.

There was no slaughter of prisoners either. A new sense of combat had taken hold of the soldiers of

Idra. They honored those who fought well against them.

"Now tell me the truth, friend," Mr. Arieson said to Hamid Khaidy. "Have you ever had so much downright fun in your life?"

"It's more than fun," said Khaidy. "It is life itself."

"I knew you'd see it that way. Now, how do you feel about fighting the Israelis in the Negev?"

"Just make sure we don't have to battle some out-of-shape reservists. I want their standing army," said Khaidy.

He did not even ask how Mr. Arieson planned to get them into position against one of the most heavily defended countries per square foot in the world.

In Washington the word was ominous. A nuclear-attack carrier had fallen into the hands of one of the zaniest countries in the world, which had devoted its military efforts to bombing kosher restaurants in Paris, kidnapping American priests, and trying to buy an atomic bomb to make it an Islamic bomb. Now it had a carrier full of nuclear weapons, had penetrated the U.S. Sixth Fleet, and could, if it knew how to fly the planes and use the equipment, probably slip a warhead right into Washington, D.C. Or anywhere else in the world it wanted.

And General Mohammed Moomas wanted lots of places. He wanted just about any place with good plumbing and a lack of infestation by tsetse flies; he wanted what were better known as the second and first worlds.

The question was, and it was a hard one, should the United States sink its own nuclear aircraft carrier? The decision fell on the President alone.

"I'm not going to kill American boys just yet. I've got other ways to deal with this," he said.

In Folcroft Sanitarium, Harold W. Smith got the call for help.

"If ever we've needed you before, we need you now. Get your people onto the ship and take it back," came the President's voice.

"Well, I can't commit them just yet."

"Why not?"

"Both of them have gone back to their Korean town."

"Well, call them out of it. Tell them it's more important than anything they've ever done."

"I'll try. But I think they've quit."

"Quit? They can't quit. Not now. No. They can't quit." The President's normally modulated and calm voice began to rise.

"Who is going to stop them, Mr. President?"

"Well, beg. Do anything. Offer them anything. Give them California if you have to. We'll lose it anyhow to that maniac Mohammed Moomas."

"I'll try, sir," said Harold W. Smith, as the civilized world hunkered down for the onslaught.

The wedding of Poo Cayang and the white Master of Sinanju could not be disturbed by an urgent message, not even one from America, where the Masters of Sinanju were now serving.

It was a sacred time for a Master to be married, said the baker in broken, halting English. He was answering Chiun's special phone on this day because Chiun, as everyone knew, considered the white his son, and therefore he was the father of the groom.

As was custom, four bags of barley were brought to the center of the home of the baker and were opened and trod upon by all the guests. Pigs were being roasted and their fresh crisp aroma tickled the nostrils of all those present, even the honored Masters of Sinanju, whom everyone knew did not eat pork, but only the weakest portions of the rice.

From this village had come the great Masters of Sinanju, and now with the beautiful Poo Cayang joining herself to the white Master, everyone could be assured the line would continue. And if the line would continue, then the village would be assured of a livelihood without ever really having to work very hard.

The Masters had brought sustenance to everyone for thousands of years and now they could be assured of thousands more. The white blood could be bred out within a generation or two. But even that did not matter.

Korea had lived through rule by Mongols and Chinese and Japanese. Only rarely had they ever ruled themselves. Except for Sinanju. No one dared rule Sinanju because of the Masters. And so when communism, another foreign idea, took hold, they knew it would pass, but what would not pass would be Sinanju.

Poo Cayang was hailed by all as she was carried through the streets of the village and then back to her house. Anyone who couldn't get inside stood outside.

Inside, Remo the white was dressed in a Western suit a tailor had hurriedly made, along with a tie, a silly white ornament. Chiun wore the traditional formal black stovepipe hat and white kimono.

He received the traditional assurances from the parents that their precious Poo was a virgin.

"Of course she's a virgin," Remo whispered. "Who would do it to her of his own free will?"

"You are talking about the woman who is going to be your wife, the mother of your child," said Chiun.

"Don't remind me," said Remo.

Poo entered and the floor creaked. The mother smiled to Remo. The father smiled to Remo. Chiun smiled back.

A priest from a larger neighboring village had been brought in. He bound their wrists in white cloth. Poo pledged obedience and good spirit and whatever dowry she brought. Remo just said:

"I do."

Since Remo was Western, they all said he should perform the Western custom of kissing the bride. Poo lifted her moon-shaped face and closed her eyes. Remo gave her a peck on the cheek.

"That's not a Western kiss," she said.

"How would you know? You never left Sinanju," said Remo.

"I'll show you a Western kiss," said Poo, reaching up to Remo's neck and pulling her face close to his. She pummeled her lips into his and thrust her tongue into his mouth, passionately searching for his.

It felt like some giant-muscled clam was trying to eat Remo's gums. He slipped free and out of respect to the bridal party refrained from spitting.

"Where did you learn that?" asked Remo.

"I read a lot," said Poo.

"Then practice tonight. I've got work. Is the wedding over?"

"There are other things you are supposed to do, Remo," said Poo. "Other bridal things that I am entitled to."

"You got everything in the prenuptial agreement," said Remo.

"I am talking about things that are understood," she said. "Things that don't have to be mentioned."

"Everything has to be mentioned," said Remo. "That's why there are contracts. The two hundred bolts of silk will be delivered in a couple of days."

"She's right, Remo. You owe her certain duties," said Chiun.

"You're interfering in my marriage," said Remo.

"Did you think I wouldn't?" asked Chiun. He was puzzled by this. Remo had known him more than twenty years now. What a silly thing for him to say. Not only was he going to interfere with the marriage but he was going to make sure the son was raised right. And Remo should expect that.

"Then if you care to interfere, you can fulfill the marriage obligations."

"I have done my job for Sinanju. Now it is your turn, Remo," he said, and turning to the guests, Chiun asked for tolerance.

"He has known only white women, generally consorting with the worst scum of womankind. They have gotten to his brain. I am sure that as he grows to know and revere our precious Poo, he will respond in a natural and correct way."

"He's supposed to do things on the wedding night," said Poo.

"It doesn't say so in the contract."

"Every wedding agreement implies that," said Poo.

"Now, you know, dear," said Chiun to Poo, "what I have had to live with lo these twenty-some years."

There was a grumble among the guests. Part of the grumble was the floorboards creaking under Poo's feet. She had a habit of stamping when she got mad.

"Not that I'm complaining," said Chiun.

"A Master never complains," said the baker, Poo's father. Everyone agreed that Chiun did not complain.

"Some would say I have reason to complain, but I have chosen not to. After all, what good does complaining do?" he asked everyone assembled.

They all agreed, except Remo.

"You love to complain, Little Father. Your day without a complaint would be hell," said Remo.

Everyone agreed Remo was an ungrateful son, especially Poo.

"Whether you believe me or not, he likes to complain and he knows it," said Remo. "And someday I am going to be the sole Master of Sinanju, and let me tell you all right now: I'm taking down names."

Chiun gasped, wounded to the core. What ingratitude! What malevolence! But what really astounded Chiun so much was that somewhere and somehow, Remo had picked up a knowledge of what would work in the village of Sinanju. Threats always worked, and keeping score was the best way to make them do so. The grumbling stopped. Poo began crying, and Remo walked out of the baker's house into the muddy streets and up the hill to the great House of Sinanju.

It was empty inside. Remo had remembered it full, with treasure stacked on treasure, bowls of pearls, beautiful statues, and gold in coins minted by sovereign countries that no longer even existed. He had been amazed when he first saw it, how fresh the coins looked. How perfect the statues were. It was a historical treasure, untouched and unused. So Sinanju, he felt, really didn't lose anything it needed, rather something that was a poignant reminder of how long this house of assassins had existed.

He would, if he could, get the treasure back, but he knew he couldn't, and his real gift to Chiun and the Masters of which he was a part was doing his service to perfection. That was the legacy of Sinanju. That was the real treasure. What he knew and what his body knew.

The scrolls had been laid out for Remo. He was fairly certain Mr. Arieson would be in some Swedish

scroll, since the name was definitely Swedish or
Danish.

But the Nordic scrolls, the time of service to the
Viking kings by the Masters of Sinanju, were nowhere to be seen. Instead there were the scrolls of
Rome and Greece from 2,000 B.C. to A.D. 200. Remo
went over them again, looking for an Arieson. There
were recorded tributes, recorded services, recorded
prices, a comment on a new peculiar religion coming
out of Judea which the current Master of the time
said had no future because it appealed to slaves.

He had advised one of the followers of the new
sect to change a few things to make it popular. Make
it appeal to the rich, not the poor. No one was ever
going to get anywhere saying, "Blessed are the poor."

It was this lengthy commentary that Chiun had
marked, the analysis of good religions and bad ones.
The religion of the Rabbi Jesus would never succeed
because:

One, it did not appeal to the rich and powerful.

Two, followers were not promised power and
earthly goods.

Three, there was no place in it for a good assassin.
After all, what could one do with a sect that was
supposed to love its enemies?

Fortunately, as later scrolls showed, time healed
that and Christians could be every bit as good em-
ployers for an assassin as everyone else. But at first,
especially during its rise in the second century, Christianity had given Sinanju a scare.

And then of course there were the ancient cults of
Dionysus and Isis, Mithraism, which also gave Sinanju
a scare, and absolutely not one word of a Mr. Arieson,
or any description of a man who could let projectiles
pass through him. No one could do that. Yet Remo
had seen it at Little Big Horn.

Remo knew Chiun was coming up the pathway to the great House of Sinanju.

He could tell the light movement of the body, the silence of the footsteps, the unity of the being that now entered the big empty house, once storage for tribute of the ages.

"The treasures of Sinanju," said Chiun.

"I know," said Remo. "They're gone."

"Only when we get them back will we be able to deal with Mr. Arieson. Until then may the world watch out."

"Since when have you cared about the world, Little Father?"

"I care about a world we may not be able to find work in."

"There's always work for an assassin."

"Not always," said Chiun, and would say no more, other than that Harold W. Smith had called for Remo and Chiun, and Chiun had told him he was not leaving Sinanju anymore.

"I think I will," said Remo.

"You owe something to Poo, precious Poo. Poo Cayang Williams. It is a funny last name. She asks if she must keep it."

"Tell her she doesn't have to keep anything."

The telephone line had been set up in the baker's house for the wedding and Remo entered the house amid the stares of a hostile family. He smiled at the parents. They turned away coldly. He smiled at Poo. She broke down in tears. The phone was off the hook.

"Hello, Smitty, Remo here. If you say it's an emergency, then I'll just have to go."

"Thank goodness. What changed your mind, Remo?"

"No change of mind. Duty first."

"I don't care what changed your mind. We have a problem. The USS *Polk*, with all hands on board and full of nuclear weapons, has been seized by the world's number-one lunatic, General Mohammed Moomas. We don't know how he did it, but he's got nuclear weapons at his command now. The Pentagon has retreated to its deep shelters beneath the Rockies, and the rest of the Sixth Fleet has surrounded the carriers, and atomic subs are waiting to make a pass. But we don't want to lose those men. Can you get in there and save them?"

"That's not the place you want to get hit. I'm going to go right for the head."

"Moomas?"

"Exactly."

"What if he's not afraid to die?"

"I'll find something, Smitty."

"How come you're so anxious now, Remo?"

"Not anxious. As a matter of fact, I hate to leave home, and if so many innocent lives weren't at stake, I'd never go out."

"You know, you sound married, Remo."

Remo hung up, and with greater gravity he told Poo that only his service to his beloved country could be enough to make him leave Sinanju on his blessed wedding night. Even as he spoke, he realized how Chiun had learned to facilitate untruths so well. He had been married for forty years.

In Korean, Poo said that was all right. She was going to go with him.

"I can't take you with me, it's dangerous," said Remo.

"Who can be in danger when protected by a Master of Sinanju?" asked Poo with a smile.

Her parents nodded.

"And if we should get a moment alone"—Poo

smiled—"why then, who knows what we shall do on our honeymoon." The smile became a grin and the grin became a laugh, and her parents packed her trunks and when the American helicopter arrived to take him to the American ship that would take him to the American plane, her luggage totaled fifteen large crates.

"What's that?" asked Remo, pointing to a crate the size of a small car.

"That, dear Remo, is our wedding bed. You wouldn't want us to leave on our honeymoon without our wedding bed."

By the time Remo arrived in Idra he was ready to kill before asking questions. He was ready to kill because it was morning, or possibly because it was hot. He did not care which.

He had left Poo in friendly Jerusalem, to pick her up when he got out of Idra. That she accepted as a necessity, provided he came right back.

Poo, a simple little girl from a Korean fishing village, settled for the suite at the Hotel David that Henry Kissinger used when he did shuttle diplomacy. Anwar Sadat had used it also. So had President Nixon. Poo said it would be fine provided she could possibly have another apartment for her personal effects. Remo left Poo to the United States State Department, which Smith had enlisted for him. He told the chargé d'affaires to give her whatever she wanted. He asked if American diplomats ever performed special services for deserving Americans.

"Sometimes," he had been told.

Remo mentioned wedding-night duties.

The chargé d'affaires declined.

Remo flew to Egypt, then boarded a plane for Morocco, and took a Moroccan flight into the capital of nearby Idra.

Idra had three times signed a nation-merging treaty
with Morocco. In between it waged war against that
state as a traitor to the Arab cause. General Mohammed Moomas listed Aden through Syria as organizations loyal to the Arab cause, including at one time
or another every faction of the Palestine Liberation
Organization.

Currently Morocco was considered in pan-Arabic
unity with Idra, and therefore allowed to land planes.
Remo was told that with his American passport he
was going to have trouble in Idra.

"No I won't," said Remo.

When the customs clerk at the Idra International
Airport asked to see Remo's passport, Remo killed
him.

That was what marriage had done to his temper.
He beat the clerk's rolling head out of the airport's
doorway amid his sudden very loud welcome to the
foremost nation struggling against Zionism, imperialism, and the Islamic way of life. No one else asked
to see his passport.

In fact, the major part of the army was gone from
Idra and the General was alone with a few guards
around his palace, morosely listening to the news of
the seizure of the USS *Polk* from the U.S. Navy.

The Arab world was aflame with the news. Here
was a truly great victory of courage and skill against
a formidable foe. The soldiers had shown daring
and brilliance that had even won the respect of their
enemies. No longer were they just the darlings of
left-wing academics and Nazis.

They were even respected by their foes.

The response was dizzying. People didn't run out
into the street like angry mobs or even fire off guns
in joy. Rather a new respect was sweeping through

the Arab world, a confidence they had not known since Sal a Din.

Remo chased a guard away from the gate and was sorry there was no fight. He stormed in on a vast marble-floored perfumed room called the "Suicide Revolutionary Command Bunker."

The General, in a white suit with enough medals to have participated in fifteen major wars and a landslide, sat glumly listening to the announcers glorify his name as one of the greatest Arab leaders of all time.

Remo grabbed a handful of his curly black hair and shook him. Some of the medals fell off, making clinking sounds on the marble.

"Are you one of his men too?" said the General. "You've finally come to kill me."

"I've come to get back my carrier."

"I don't have it," said the General. Remo gave his neck a short twist between forefinger and thumb, pinching a nerve.

The General cried out.

"I don't control them anymore. I don't control them anymore."

"Well, try, sweetheart. I'm sure you can set up communications to the USS *Polk*."

"I already have, but they don't listen to me."

"Try again," said Remo. While servants ran to neighboring rooms to bring in communications equipment—the suicide command bunker was only equipped with liquor and food—Remo polished a bit of the marble with the General's face.

He would have killed him, but he needed him to talk. Remo even hated the walls. If he didn't watch out, the dangerous emotion of rage would take away his concentration, and without that he could just as easily kill himself as someone else with some of his moves.

It was the mind that made Sinanju Sinanju.

Finally the equipment was brought in and the General, weeping, got through to the USS *Polk* and a colonel he recognized as Hamid Khaidy.

"Faithful brother, we command you to speak to a beloved guest."

"We're busy," came back the voice.

"What are you doing?"

"We're activating the nuclear warheads. We're in range of Jerusalem and we can penetrate their air cover."

The General put his hand over the receiver.

"Should I ask them to stop?"

"Hold on," said Remo. "We've got to think about that one."

6

"No. I'd better stop that one," said Remo after a moment. He thought of Jerusalem going up in a nuclear cloud. It was a sacred place to all three monotheistic religions and home to one of them. And besides, precious Poo was under his protection; it had been announced in the village that she had nothing to fear because she was leaving with a Master.

Chiun would never forgive him if she got hurt.

Was he going to save this sacred city, capital of a dear American ally, just because Chiun would hold it against him? Had he lost so much of his moral bearings? Had the work of the nuns in the Newark orphanage been so replaced by Sinanju that he would hardly give a second thought to the fact that Jerusalem was where Christianity was born?

Had it gone that far?

Long ago, thought Remo.

"Tell him you are sending an emissary to help."

"You will help, of course?"

"They don't need help, apparently," said Remo.

"What can one man do?"

"I'm here, ain't I?" said Remo, nodding back at the wounded at the entrance of the luxurious suicide command center.

"Can we come to an accommodation?" asked the General.

"No."

"What would you take to make sure those top officers never set foot on shore again?"

Remo smiled. He knew what was happening, but he pretended to be the innocent American.

"You want 'em dead?" asked Remo, feigning surprise.

"I am faced with a problem you might not understand. Of course I am the foremost battler against imperialism, Zionism, oppression, and capitalism, as I am against atheism. I fight for the Islamic way of life," said the General, taking a thoughtful sip of his Scotch and soda, which was as forbidden a substance to a Moslem as pork to a Jew. "But to lead the fight, one must not have someone else winning more victories. I cannot afford a stronger battler against these evils than I. Do you understand?"

"Golly, no."

"Let us suppose they defeat the Zionist entity in the sacred homeland of the Palestinians."

"You'll rejoice."

"Of course. A great and wonderful victory. Unfortunately, it will not be mine. It will be theirs. First Jerusalem will be theirs, then who knows? Damascus? Riyadh? Cairo? Where will they stop?"

"What are you saying?"

"I feel safe, on behalf of the struggling masses against Zionism, the independent Arab and Islamic nations working for Allah to restore our rightful sovereignty over Jerusalem and all of Palestine, to offer you any price to make sure those on the USS *Polk*, the heroic Arab strugglers for justice, never set foot on land."

"Kill them?"

"Any price, and I guarantee you will have the support of every Arab government. We are not poor, you know."

"There is something I want, General," said Remo, and from memory, from the droned recitations of the histories of Sinanju, he listed all the tributes he could remember, all that had been stolen while he was away doing the work of CURE.

"Even for a beginning price, this is astronomical," said the General realistically.

"No. All I want is any one of them, and for you to tell me where you got it. I'll get the rest."

The General promised undying love, and hoped the American and his own renegade soldiers would fight to the death. Then he wouldn't be obliged to search for such an extraordinary list of valuables.

The American certainly was no fool. He had been holding out for a treasure.

Once the American was off on an Idran plane to the USS *Polk*, now named the *Jihad*, or holy war, the General contacted the ship again and got Hamid Khaidy on the phone.

The General was about to play another card. He was not a leader of the struggle because he slept all day.

"Beloved colonel," he said, "I am looking for a new commander of all my armies."

"No," came back the voice of the colonel.

"What?"

"No deals. I am a soldier, not some dealer in promotions. I have fought an honorable battle. If I become a general, I will earn it on the field of honor."

"Of course I am talking about honor, the honor of being a field marshal."

"You obviously want me to set up someone, and I'm not going to do it. I will meet whatever enemy I

have face to face, and live or die by what I can do
with my courage and martial skills. No more schem-
ing. No more baby killing. No more parking a car
with a bomb at a supermarket and claiming some
great Arab victory. I am going to live and die as a
man, as a soldier, as an Arab soldier. Do you know
what that is, General?"

"I stand enlightened, brother. Your courage and
honor shame me. Let me express my support for
your new stand to your second in command."

When the General got another colonel, he whispered into the phone:

"Colonel Khaidy has gone crazy. He is talking about
getting you all killed. I authorize you to seize command from him immediately and I am promoting
you to general as of now. This is an inviolate order."

"I'm not stabbing my brother in the back," said the
other colonel. "If I get a promotion, it will be for
killing enemies, not Arabs."

"So true. So true," said the General, and asked if
there was anyone else near the phone. To twelve
men he offered supreme command of the Idran
forces, and twelve men refused him, talking about
honor, not as a normal word of conversation to make
a point, but taking it to some ridiculous extreme.
They were going to live by it.

As a last resort he tried the colonel who had caused
all this trouble in the beginning. And Colonel, now
General, Arieson was most pleased to learn that a
thin American with high cheekbones and dark eyes
was now flying toward him on an Idran plane that
was going to attempt to land on his decks.

"He wanted to kill you, and how, I thought, could
I protect our greatest victory but to warn you of his
impending arrival? I am showing you I am saving
you by sending him on a defenseless plane. And to

show my good faith, I made sure it was not flown by a Russian, but an Idran hero commander ace pilot. They may not even reach your deck."

"And in return?"

"Hold off your attack against Jerusalem and meet with other Arab leaders. I will make you commander of all our victorious forces. You may be the ruler of the Arab world."

There was only laughter at the other end of the phone.

"But you don't understand. I have what I want. I don't want the world. I want my war, my good old-fashioned war."

"Struggle, of course. It ennobles the soul. But a war must have a purpose, brother General Arieson."

"It is the purpose, brother struggler," laughed General Arieson, and hung up.

Remo learned almost immediately why the Idran air force, with the most modern jets money could buy, was ignored by the General in favor of hijacking of civilian airliners, machine-gunning of kosher restaurants, and bombing of discotheques where American servicemen danced.

He was two thousand feet up, and still rising in Russia's most advanced fighter jet, when the pilot in the front seat of the two-seater jet asked him how he was doing. He asked in Russian. Remo only remembered bits of archaic Russian needed to understand Sinanju's many years of service to the czars.

"I guess you did all right," he answered in that language.

"Do you want to take over now?" asked the pilot. He was a hero, with medals for shooting down countless enemy planes—according to the publicity, fifty Israeli, twenty American, and ten British to be exact. Actually, under cover of diplomatic protection he had shot a British bobby from an Idran embassy, and when he was ejected from that country, given credit for shooting down British fliers in fair combat.

"No, that's all right," said Remo. "You're doing fine."

The blue sky over the tight canopy made him feel part of the clouds. It was true what they said about an advanced fighter. It was a weapon strapped to the body. He did not like the weapon because it was not his body. But he could see how it would enhance the crude unrhymed moves of the average person to make him forceful. Cut a corner at Mach 3 like an off ramp. Bang, turn, and you were gone into the clouds.

"Did you like my takeoff?" asked the pilot.

"It was fine," said Remo.

"Don't you think I should have throttled forward more?"

"I don't know," said Remo.

"I felt too much resistance. That's why I asked."

"I don't know," said Remo.

"You didn't feel the lack of throttle?"

"What throttle?"

"Aren't you my Russian adviser?"

"No. I'm your passenger."

"Eeeah," screamed the pilot. "Who will land the aircraft?"

"You can't land?"

"I can. I know I can. I've done it in the trainer, but I've never done it without a Russian at the controls behind me."

"If you can, you can," said Remo.

"Not on a carrier."

"You can."

"That's special training."

"I'll show you how," said Remo.

"How can you show me how if you don't know how?"

"I didn't say I didn't know how, I just don't know how to fly the plane."

"That makes absolutely no sense!" screamed the pilot.

"Don't worry," said Remo. "It'll work. Just make a pass at the carrier."

Before they reached the carrier, they had to fly over the entire Sixth Fleet, which sent up planes to look them over. The American pilots flew nerve-shatteringly close.

"Don't think about them. Don't let them bother you."

"How can I not think about them?"

"I'll teach you a trick. I'll teach you how to land the aircraft also."

"But you've never flown one, you said."

"Never," said Remo.

"You are crazy."

"I'm alive and I intend to stay alive. Now, the first thing you have to do is notice the sky."

"It's filled with American planes flown by pilots who not only know how to fly by themselves but are considered the best in the world, if the Israeli pilots aren't. We are cursed with skilled enemies."

"You're not doing what I said. Look at the sky. See the sky. Feel the clouds, feel the moisture, be the moisture, be the clouds, be the sky."

"Yes, I can almost do that."

"Breathe. Think about your breath. Think about breathing in and breathing out."

"I do. It is good. Oh, it is good."

"Of course. Now, don't think about the planes."

"I just did."

"Of course," said Remo.

"I don't understand."

"I dare you not to think about a yellow elephant. You'll think yellow elephant. But when I tell you to think about your breath, you automatically don't think about the other planes."

"Yes, that's so."

"Your breath is vital," said Remo. "Be with your breath," and he saw the man's shoulders slump ever so slightly, indicating the muscles were relaxing, and now the man's skills could begin to take over. Remo brought him out to the sky, out to the clouds, and when they saw the pitching, bobbing little stamp of a carrier deck beneath them, he carefully avoided talking about landing and made the deck a friend, not an object of terror.

One of the most difficult feats in all aviation is landing on a pitching carrier deck, but the pilot was down before he knew it. Precisely before he knew it. If he had known he was landing the aircraft instead of joining the plane strapped around him to a friend whose motions he understood and felt, he would have either crashed or pulled up in panic.

Their plane was immediately surrounded by armed Idran soldiers, but they were not hiding behind their weapons like the guards at the palace. There was something different about these men. They were anxious to grapple with anyone who dared cause trouble.

That was what Remo had noticed about the Ojupa at Little Big Horn. It was Arieson's handiwork. He was sure of it.

And the beauty of an aircraft carrier was that there were no dust storms. This was a manmade thing of steel corners and traps. Arieson and his strange body would not be able to escape in dust this time.

"Ariseon. Arieson. I'm looking for Arieson," said Remo.

"Ah, the general," said one of the soldiers.

"Where is he?"

"Wherever he wants to be. We never know where he is," said the soldier.

Because he had landed in an Idran plane, Remo was accepted as one of the Idran Russian advisers. No one believed the pilot had landed it himself, being a brother Idran. They told him they had found a new way of fighting, using their courage and not machines.

Remo searched the hangars beneath decks. He found the American captain a prisoner in his own cabin. He found marines disarmed but treated well. He found American fliers and servicemen under guard, but nowhere was Arieson.

Finally he took the Idran soldier who had been guiding him around and said:

"I got bad news for you. I'm an American."

"Then die, enemy," said the Idran, and brought up his short-nosed automatic weapon, firing well and accurately right at Remo's midsection. And he was rather quick about it too, for a soldier.

But he was still a soldier. Remo blended him into the bulkhead.

"We're taking over this ship," he said to the marines watching.

"These guys are tough," said the marine.

"So are you," said Remo.

"Damned right," said the marine.

Remo freed the sailors the same way and then the pilots. The battle started in the main hangars and spread up to the control tower. Bodies littered the passageways. Gunfire ricocheted off the metal walls, spinning sparks and death at every level. The two sides fought from midday until midnight, when the last Idran, with his last bullet, charged at a marine with a hand grenade. The hand grenade won.

From the loudspeaker system came a voice:

"I love it. I love all you wonderful guys. You're my kind of men. Here's to you, valiant warriors."

It was Arieson. Moving along the deck was like skating on oil, so thick was the blood. Most of the living could hardly stand. Remo squished up a gory stairwell. It had been carnage. This is what Chiun had meant when he referred to the butchery of war. None of the men were really in control of themselves, rather fighting their own terror and forcing themselves to function as soldiers. It was like a butcher shop.

Arieson was laughing. Remo found him in the captain's control room.

"Now, *this* is war," he said with a grin as wide as a parade.

"And this is good-bye," said Remo.

He didn't wait for Arieson to commit, he didn't explore, he got Arieson with the steel cabin wall behind him and put two clean blows right into his midsection, the second to catch whatever lightning move Arieson had made to escape in the dust back at Little Big Horn.

Both blows struck.

They met iron. But not the steel of the captain's control room. Remo found himself with his hands piercing a helmet with a red plume on top and a burnished steel chest protector.

In Jerusalem, an archaeologist identified them for

him as a helmet and cuirass prevalent in the Mediterranean for centuries before Christ. What puzzled the archaeologist was why anyone would make them new today.

"These are brand new. Look at the forge marks. Look, some of the wax from the lost wax method is still in some of the finer scrollwork."

"I saw that."

"I would say these are fakes. But they use a method of manufacture that has been lost for centuries. How did you make them?"

"I didn't," said Remo.

"Where did you get them?"

"A friend gave them to me."

"What could have made these holes in them?" asked the archaeologist, examining the implosions in the burnished steel.

"That was done by hand," said Remo.

Back at the Hotel David, precious Poo had learned two more words in English.

"Condominium, Bloomingdale's," said Poo. She had just met some lovely New York women who felt sorry for her that she had no Western clothes. They had bought a few rags in Jerusalem. There was a small bill for Remo. Eighteen thousand dollars.

"How do you spend eighteen thousand dollars on clothes in a country whose main product is a submachine gun?" asked Remo.

"I had nothing," said Poo. "I didn't even have my husband for the blessed bridal night."

"Spend," said Remo.

"Money can't make up for love," said Poo.

"Since when?" said Remo.

"Since I don't have a condominium and a charge account at Bloomingdale's," said Poo.

Downstairs there was a message at the desk for Remo. It had come from Ireland.

The message was:

"I'm waiting for you, boyo."

Remo got the American embassy to use a special line to reach Sinanju through submarines in the West Korea Bay. This with the help of Smith of course.

"Little Father," said Remo. "Did you leave a message for me at the King David Hotel?"

"King David was a terrible ruler. The Jews are well rid of him. Fought wars. When he could have used an assassin in the Bathsheba affair, he chose war instead. Got her husband killed in battle. And what happened? Ended up in the Bible. That's what happens when you use war instead of an assassin."

"I take it you didn't leave the message."

"Every moment you are not searching for the lost treasure, you're wasting your time. Why should I waste time with you?"

"That's all I wanted to know. Thanks," said Remo.

"Has Poo conceived yet?"

"Not unless she's made it with a Hasid."

"You're not living up to your end of the bargain," said Chiun.

"I didn't say when I would consummate the marriage. I just said I would."

In Belfast, as the British armored cars rolled by, keeping Catholics and Protestants from killing themselves, and as some of the heavier participants waited in jail for the British to leave so that they could get on with the murderous religious strife that had boiled along for centuries, a man in a loose gray jacket and a worn stevedore's cap sauntered into a pub, bought everyone a round of drinks, and said:

"Here's to Hazel Thurston, long may the beloved

Prime Minister of England rule over all. To your health, boys."

Glasses flew across the bar. Some men cursed. Others drew revolvers. But the stranger just smiled.

He downed his stout in a gulp and boomed a belch that could extinguish a thousand war fires on a thousand murky heaths.

"Boyos," he said. "Would you be cursin' our beloved Prime Minister what's been hated here by both Protestant and Catholic alive lo these many years? Is that what I'm hearing?"

There was a gunshot in the Pig's Harp pub. It missed the target.

The stranger raised a hand.

"What are you shooting at me for if you hate her so much? Why don't you shoot her?"

"Yer daft, man. The bitch is better protected than the bloody crown jewels, I'm sayin'."

"So what do you do? Fire a random shot at some bobby in a soldier's uniform?"

"We do what we want, jocko," said one of the larger men at the bar.

"No. You don't," said the stranger. "Beggin' your pardon, me lad. You don't. Not a whit. Not a hair. Not a follicle on that pale British puss do you do harm to."

"Do you want to step outside and say that?" the stranger was asked.

"What for? I'm sayin' it in here."

"Then maybe, jocko, you'll just end up with a big hole in your head right here."

"Why not, boyo? Certainly keep you from doin' harm to Her Excellency the Prime Minister, Hazel Thurston. You can add another number to the deaths in Northern Ireland, and then go to the Maze Prison

and conduct the latest in great Irish tactics. Starvin'
yourself to death. Now ain't that a thing for a brave
Irishman to be doin' with his body, peelin' his own
flesh down to the bone so's all that's left is gauntness
lookin' back at that English bitch who couldn't care
less if every boyeen in Belfast gave up the ghost the
same way."

"Who are you, stranger?"

"I'm someone who remembers the great Irish wars,
when you fought with ax and sword and shield like
the honorable men you always were. I'm talkin' of
the blessed battle of the Boyne, where English and
Irishmen fought like men. What do you do today?
You invade a neighbor's living room and shoot up
his dinner, along with his guests and family. What's
wrong with you, boyo? Are you an Irishman or a
Swede?"

"Why are you talking about Swedes?"

"You can't get a war out of them today if you
stand on your head."

"We don't want a war with them. We got enough
war already in Belfast."

"No. That's just the trouble, boyo. You don't," said
the stranger. "If you had a war, a real war, an old-
fashioned war, you'd march out to the grandest music you ever heard, and face your enemy square on
one day, not three hundred and sixty-five including
Christmas and the Feast of the Immaculate Concep-
tion. You'd have it out. Over and done with. Winner
take all and blessings to the loser. But what do you
have now?"

"We got unemployment," said one.

"We got streets filled with glass," said another.

"We got all the garbage of war and none of its
fruits. We're left out again," said a third.

"Right," said the stranger. "What you got to do

now is get Britain out of Northern Ireland so both sides can kill each other in peace."

"Never happen," said one.

"We been tryin' for four hundred years."

"You been doin' it wrong," said the stranger. "You been shootin' here and shootin' there, when you only need to get one lady."

"Miss Hazel Thurston," yelled one of the men at the end of the bar.

"Exactly," said the stranger.

"You can't get near her."

"Who'd want to?" said another.

"I not only know how you can get to her, but where you could put her until the bloody British get their bloody arses off true Irish soil."

"You make a lot of talk, stranger. Let's see you do it."

"Well, come with me and I will," said the stranger.

"One last drink."

"You've had your last drink. Now you're going to have yourselves a British prime minister," said the stranger. "Allow me to introduce myself. My name's Arieson."

"That's hardly a McGillicuddy or an O'Dowd."

"It's a fine old name," said the stranger. "You'll learn to love me. Most men do, but they won't admit it nowadays."

Protecting the Prime Minister of England were not only Scotland Yard and several branches of British intelligence, but a group of terrorist experts who surrounded this great lady with a shield that had never been broken. It was they who, in the last minute, moved her from a hotel room downstairs to the dining room just before her bedroom blew up.

What they had, and what the terrorists did not

know, was a simple little code that three times out of five could pick up a terrorist target.

It had come from the same great minds that had cracked the German codes in the first days of the Second World War.

It had come from the simple and brilliant British logic that had produced so much good reason in the world. While the terrorist acts might appear random, most were brutally logical and planned from a central source: a KGB office in Moscow.

Despite all the various grievances on different continents in different civilizations, if one simply stepped back from the local complaints and looked at the broad picture, every international terrorist organization was directed against Western interests. None was directed against Communist-bloc countries, where grievances were often greater.

It was a war directed against the populations of the West.

Given that one office in the KGB directed this worldwide network, or at least trained its leaders, then certain techniques had to be standard. There had to be an operational fingerprint. What would appear to be random acts were not.

Knowing there had to be a pattern, the men of British special intelligence formed a broad picture of every incident and put it on a graph, and almost like a production chart did they see a pattern emerge, especially for the IRA, since it was taken over by ostensibly radical Marxists not aligned with Russia.

While they could not protect every target without giving their knowledge away, this special group could most certainly protect the royal family and the Prime Minister.

Thus, when Prime Minister Hazel Thurston's bedroom was about to be blown up, they could move her out of it.

Thus, this day while the Prime Minister was taking a short vacation near Bath and its supposedly curative waters, they detoured her party off a main road.

"Another attack?" asked Prime Minister Thurston. She was pale, with a proud, almost aristocratic face, despite the fact she had been born of middle-class merchants in the shires.

Her special aide looked at his watch.

"I would estimate within two minutes on the normal route," he said.

"You have it down that well?" she asked.

"Sometimes," he said with classic British calm.

Two minutes and fifteen seconds later, while the Prime Minister's little protected caravan cruised a narrow back road between golden fields, under a rare and blessed British sun, a muffled boom was heard far off on the main highway.

"I suppose that's them," she said.

"Should be," said her intelligence aide.

"I do hope no one was hurt," she said, and went back to her papers. This was sheep country, and on the back roads, as they had for centuries, the British herders moved their flocks and slowed traffic. The sheep took priority over Rolls-Royces—even government Rolls-Royces.

A herder, his tweed cap weathered by sun and rain, saw who was being delayed, and with his crook in hand came over to the large black car to apologize.

Hazel Thurston smiled. This was the salt of England. The good farmer stock. Did their work. Kept their peace, and when called on, always filled the ranks of Britain's armies. She had known this sort of men from her father's store. Not a one of them was not good for what he owed.

She knew her people and they knew her. The Prime Minister lowered her window. As the herder bent down, so did his staff. It had an opening in the top, rather curious when one looked at it, because this staff happened to have rifling. The herder cleared up the puzzle by explaining that if the British bitch didn't do exactly as he said, a more than wee little bullet was going to come out of the barrel of that staff and blow her bloody British brains all over her intelligence chaps and her official Rolls-Royce.

she knew her people and they knew her. The Prime Minister lowered her window. As the limou-

7

"You'll never get away with it," said the Prime Minister. "You simply can't hide a British prime minister on English soil. There aren't places to hide. Now, if you surrender this moment, I will be lenient."

Hazel Thurston looked around the spacious room. It was forty feet by forty feet, with clean stone walls on every side. It had once had windows, but these were sealed by something dark. In fact, the only light came from a single light bulb powered by a generator. It was dank, but the whole country was dank at this time of year. She knew generally where they were, just outside Bath. She had clocked it. They hadn't traveled more than fifteen minutes. And people at the old stone Roman aqueduct nearby had waved to her just before the herder had stuck that gun in her face and blindfolded her.

There was absolutely no way they could hide her within fifteen minutes of a British city. It could not be done.

Already, she and her intelligence aide knew, all traffic in the area was being stopped and searched. Anyone who was not certain to belong in the area was being brought in for questioning.

The intelligence people would search every room,

closet, alley, ash can, cellar, attic, belfry, and pew within fifty miles.

"It's probably only minutes before our chaps get here," said the Prime Minister. "So I am giving you a last chance to be easy on yourself."

"Bugger off, we're gettin' what's due us, and this time you gotta give in," said the man who had been disguised as a herder.

There were four others in this large room. The intelligence chap had been tied up and placed in a corner.

"Young man, you're filled with your success. But it's going to be short-lived. There is absolutely no way you can hide a British prime minister so close to where she was kidnapped on British soil. It cannot be done."

"We don't need your lip. We've 'ad enough of that in Belfast, I'll be tellin' you."

"Then let me express myself in a manner you might find more understandable. If you surrender now, there will be a short jail term and you can go back to writing your dissertations on how the world should be turned upside down with us at the bottom and you at the top and running things. If you don't, sir, we will hang you by your privates until you wish you had been run over by an armored car at birth."

"Pipe down or I'll shoot your brains out."

"Well then, shoot, you pig-faced unemployable drunk."

"If you don't shut up, we'll do to you what we did to Lord Mountbatten," said the terrorist, referring to how they had killed the British war hero by planting a bomb on his boat.

"You mean you will do to me what you do to innocent passersby, British regulars trying to keep the peace, and Lord Mountbatten?"

"Bet your ass, Brit."

"What splendid company to die among," said the British Prime Minister.

Suddenly there was a laugh, a loud roar of a laugh that seemed to reverberate among the stones. The Prime Minister looked behind her. There was an entrance there, a clean stone doorway. But behind it seemed to be a dirt tunnel. And yet this was not a cellar. There was nothing about this large stone room that was cellarlike. There were many windows. Cellars did not have windows. That the windows were blocked by something did not matter. No one built a cellar with large windows.

"Spoken like a man," said the man with the beard and thick neck and blazing eyes. He wore a tweed suit and carried a briefcase and his face seemed alight with joy.

"And who are you?" asked the Prime Minister.

"Someone who admired your Falklands war. Good to see you people at it again. It's been a long time for you, eh?"

"Who are you? What do you want?"

"We want you out of Northern Ireland. Let everyone be free to do what they want."

"They want to kill each other, you know."

"You could call it that."

"What do you call it?"

"I call it the national expression of will."

"Their will is to kill each other."

"Then what do you care?"

"We have an obligation to see that this is settled peacefully. We have citizens there. We have a tradition of hundreds of years there. We do not intend to leave a tradition of massacre in that poor ravaged land."

"Busybody," said the man with the beard. "You

allowed yourselves the Falklands. Why do you deny the same joy to your citizens of Northern Ireland?"

"I don't know who you are, but may I remind you we were attacked by Argentina."

"Someone's always attacked by someone, and that someone always has some inalienable and legitimate grievance. Let the Protestants and Catholics there, in their own good way, kill themselves like Christians."

"Are you a Jew or Moslem?"

"Can be both at times, although they would be the first to deny me. I really don't get the proper respect I deserve, the way I deserve."

"Perhaps we can change that. May I first ask that you untie my intelligence aide? His wrists seem bound a bit too tight."

The man with the muscled neck waved to the herder. The Prime Minister saw her intelligence aide watch the quick way the herder responded.

Prime Minister Hazel Thurston saw him rub his wrists and then amble to one of the walls with a window and wait there, apparently innocently. But the Prime Minister knew better. Her aide never did anything innocently or casually. Everything had a purpose.

Whatever he was doing by that window had to be protected, so she distracted her captors by saying she might make a compromise.

"You disappoint me, Hazel," said the man. "I thought you were made of sterner stuff than that."

"The world of reality requires reasonable people to negotiate," she said. "Just what can we do for you?"

"Pull out of Northern Ireland. Just get your troops out and let the people decide."

"I'm afraid I can't do that. But what I will do is form another commission—"

"We'll get you out. You see, you are the only person of power in your government, and without you there as a strong leader, they'll strike a deal. It always happens when a country loses a strong leader. It's absolutely predictable. Any nation with a strong leader like yourself is weak without that leader. Strong people make others around them weak. True, and you have to know it."

"Where did you get that theory?" she asked. She saw her man had his hand behind him now, as he stood directly in front of the window. He was doing something with that hand.

"It is as eternal a fact as gravity."

The Prime Minister saw her man nod. She knew they could not talk because this strange room might be bugged. She also knew this stranger might just be right. Without her in the cabinet, her nation just might strike a deal to withdraw all troops from Northern Ireland.

The only redeeming event came when she was left alone with her intelligence aide. He opened up his hand without saying a word and then both of them smiled at each other. A dark crumbling substance filled his palm. From the open window he had taken earth. Someone had just covered this stone room with earth. It would have to show in the countryside. It would be one of the first places Scotland Yard would look. A stone house that had suddenly disappeared under a pile of earth could not possibly be overlooked, least of all in the communities around Bath.

They waited for the rescue which they expected any minute. And waited.

The problem was simple. Find one prime minister

and her intelligence aide seized outside Bath, England, that morning. The solution was just as simple.

All roads were cordoned off. Every house in every village was searched. Every hayloft, garage and alley, can, dumpster, ditch was accounted for on a big grid map by teatime, and by supper there was not a hint of a whisper of what had been done with the Prime Minister.

"She has to be here," said an inspector, who had taken time out to enjoy the refreshing springs and the baths the Romans had built here almost two thousand years before, when they had occupied the island as far north as Hadrian's wall.

The town of Bath was named after these baths. Before the Romans, the Celts, Picts, and Saxons—the general populace of the area—had not considered bathing healthy, and they had the aroma to prove it. The Romans, as clean a people as the Japanese, introduced washing to the then barbaric countryside. And specifically at Bath the waters were said to be curative. Now Scotland Yard needed the cure.

"How in bloody blue blazes do you lose a prime minister amidst a homogeneous, friendly population? We have searched every basement, boardinghouse, and hangar, and by damn, she's gone," said the inspector. "I'm sure they're going to kill her."

"Why is that?" asked the Minister of Defense.

"The demands are ridiculous. They say unless we pull out of Northern Ireland right now, she dies."

"Might not be that ridiculous," said the Minister of Defense, letting the waters soak through his pores. "The strangest development has occurred there. Add in the kidnap, and we just might make the deal."

"Give in to kidnappers?"

"Do you know what's happening in Belfast now, Inspector?"

"It certainly can't mean we would have to pull out."

"Combined with the fact that there's hardly anyone left to say no with the force of our iron Prime Minister, yes. Belfast has become not an urban guerrilla battleground but a war zone. Someone has formed a provisional wing of the provisional wing of the IRA and is actually engaging British forces in open combat and winning."

"The IRA? Can't be. They can't get fifty people together without fighting amongst themselves," said the inspector.

"A splinter group of a splinter group. And I suspect they're behind this Thurston kidnapping also. They're outfighting us in Belfast and outthinking us in Bath," said the Minister of Defense.

"Are we going to lose?"

"We may have already lost unless we can find our Prime Minister."

"They couldn't have hidden her around here. We've looked everywhere," said the inspector.

"Well, obviously there's some place you haven't looked. There's only one other choice. Call for help from the Americans."

"I'd rather lose," said the inspector.

"So would I, but we can't."

"Why not?"

"State policy. This is my ultimatum. If we don't get our prime minister by midnight, you'll have American help by morning."

Poo and Remo had returned to Sinanju from the honeymoon. Poo had brought dresses from Jerusalem, a Western city with a good ruler, more often than not.

She told her friends about hotel suites and clothes.

She told her friends about new and exotic foods. Bread made of wheat that had a snow-white center and a dark crust.

Sweet drinks like Coca-Cola.

There was even a bread with a hole in it that was very hard, and should not be eaten when it came out of the oven, but baked again after it was split open. It was a delicacy spread with a white milk-fat substance called cream cheese and then topped with fish that had been held over a burning log. All her friends made a face when Poo told them she had eaten this dish called bagels and lox.

Raw grasses called salads were also served.

There was cloth on bedding called sheets and if one rang a buzzer one could order anything one wanted to eat at any time of the day.

There were rings and necklaces. There were rooms for dining where everyone from all over the globe ate.

The roads were not as nice as the ones built coming into Sinanju from Pyongyang, but there were more cars.

"One car would be more cars," a friend said.

And when they asked her about the wedding night, she only smiled knowingly and said nothing, letting their imaginations play over the delights the white Master of Sinanju had given her. But to her mother, she told the truth. She had to. There wasn't going to be a baby.

"He didn't touch me," cried Poo. "He didn't kiss me or touch me or anything."

"Nothing?" asked the mother.

"I said 'or anything,' " cried Poo.

"Did you entice him with the tricks I taught you?"

"I did everything but lengthen it in a steel vise."

"Try the steel vise," said her mother.

"He's a Master of Sinanju. You can't get close to him if he doesn't want you to. And, Momma, he doesn't want to. He doesn't want me."

"He's got to want you. He's your husband. I'll speak to your father."

And so the baker's wife told the baker what the daughter had told the mother, and the baker, with his wife's hectoring voice telling him exactly what he should say and do, fearfully went up to the great wooden house on the hill where the Masters of Sinanju had lived for millennia.

"And don't let him squirm away," called the baker's wife.

Squirm away? thought the baker. Master Chiun could split a man's skull like a dried leaf since he was twelve. He's going to kill me. At least there is one good thing about being killed by a Master of Sinanju. He can make it faster and less painful than anything else.

The baker crushed his own hat in his hands, and bowing, mounted the old wood steps to the entrance of the House of Sinanju. Emissaries throughout history had mounted these steps. Rarely did a villager come except to ask for help with a problem that could be solved by money or swift and deadly justice.

At the door the baker took off his shoes, as was the custom before entering the house. He kissed the threshold, and with his face pressed firmly to the floor, called out:

"O great Master of Sinanju, I, the father of Poo, Baya Cayang, humbly beseech your awesome magnificence to deign to converse with me."

"Enter, Baya Cayang, father of Poo, wife of my son, Remo," came the voice of Chiun, Master of Sinanju. "And rise, for you will be the grandfather of the issue of the marriage."

Back in the streets of the village it had all been clear. The baker's wife had told him to tell Chiun in no uncertain terms that Remo had not performed as a husband. They had agreed to the marriage with a white because they were sure that anyone who was a Master, even though he was white, could perform well. In brief, the baker's family had been cheated. And Chiun should be told that clearly. Either Chiun's son must deliver on all the marriage vows, or Poo would return to the baker's home, and the baker would keep the Master's bridal purse.

It sounded so much more reasonable in the muddy streets of Sinanju than in the great house of many rooms. How was one going to tell Chiun that the white he loved more dearly than a son, the white of whom no one could dare speak even a hint of ill to Chiun's face, was not a man?

It was death, if the speaker was lucky.

But Baya Cayang knew he could not return to his home either, with Poo crying and his wife badgering him. So it was either death or living death, and Baya Cayang, after he had been given rice wine by Chiun, and had talked about the weather, and how the day was going with Chiun, brought up the subject most tenderly.

"We are honored to be the parents of Poo, who has been wed to a Master."

"The honor is ours," said Chiun. He did not particularly like the Cayangs. They were a greedy family and somewhat slothful. But at least they were from Sinanju, and when one considered all the whites Remo had run around with, Poo was a blessing.

"Like you, we eagerly await a grandson," said Cayang. He dared to offer his cup for more wine. Chiun poured it. He was gracious about giving all guests as much wine as he could foist upon them, but considered any who would take it drunkards. He himself, like Remo, could not drink. Their nervous systems would disintegrate under the influence of alcohol, such was the fineness to which they had tuned their bodies.

"No one awaits a grandson more eagerly than I," said Chiun.

What did this dolt Cayang want? They already had enough gold to buy pigs for a lifetime of feasts. He wouldn't even have to bake anymore if Chiun did not demand the fine rice cakes of the village.

"There are things that must happen for Poo to become pregnant."

"Oh, those things," said Chiun. "She could do those lying on her back."

"She can. Not that I know she can. Not that she has. She hasn't."

"Of course she hasn't. I cannot tell you how glad I am, Baya, that Remo has stopped running around with white sluts, especially a Russian. Americans are bad enough, but the Russians are worse."

"Whites go crazy over Korean men, I hear. They do strange things with their bodies."

Movement would be strange, thought Chiun, remembering his own wife. Still, what did one want from a woman but to bear children and cook the meals, and hector as little as possible? Remo, on the other hand, was immersed in white ways. This woman he might have even fallen in love with, this Russian, worked in their government and commanded men like a soldier. He thought Remo might have even married Anna Chutesov, until Poo Cayang changed things. So if the baker beat around the bush, nevertheless he had to be respected for helping save Remo from his own kind.

"Because of your lovely daughter, Baya, Remo will

never have to endure those evil onslaughts of white women."

"I hear they wear special clothes and do special things, with ointments and the like," said Baya.

"Let us not talk of the evils of white women, but the virtues of your daughter."

"O Great Chiun," wailed Baya Cayang. "She remains as untouched today as the day she and Remo left on their honeymoon."

"What are you saying?"

"I am saying, Great Chiun, neither of us will be grandfathers."

"What is wrong with Poo?"

"Nothing. Remo has not performed as a husband," said Baya, shutting his eyes, waiting for the blow. Slowly he opened them. Perhaps Chiun did not wish to kill him with his eyes closed. But all he saw when he opened his eyes was a Master of Sinanju, his wisps of hair bobbing with his head, nodding agreement with Baya Cayang, father of Poo, baker of the village, who now knew he had an excellent chance of seeing the morning.

"Remo," called out Chiun.

"What do you want?" came the voice from the large house, echoing loudly because there was no longer the great treasure to absorb and muffle the sound.

"I want you to come out here," called Chiun.

"I'm busy."

"He still has American ways of disrespect," confided Chiun. "But we will keep it in the family." And then louder Chiun yelled:

"It will only take a moment." And to Cayang he whispered:

"You would think it would break him to give us a minute. I don't know what to do with the boy. Never have. Given him the best years of my life, and now this. Well, we'll straighten it out like Koreans. We'll have a little one into Poo in no time."

"All right," said Remo, entering the room, reading a scroll. Cayang recognized Korean, but there was other writing on it also, strange writing like that in the West. But none that he had ever seen before, and he had seen an occasional American newspaper sent back to Sinanju by the Master himself for the archives of the house of assassins.

"Little Father," said Remo, "I have reread this scroll ten times, and I see nothing of Mr. Arieson. There are Greeks fighting Persians and Greeks fighting each other, there are religious rites, Olympic games, poems, a description of a drunken feast in honor of the god Bacchus, and the payment of statuary along with gold. What am I supposed to be seeing?"

"You wouldn't see your nose in front of your face, even your big white one," said Chiun.

"All right. I have a big white nose. Now tell me what's going on."

"What didn't go on is the question," said Chiun.

Remo saw Poo's father. He nodded hello.

"Poo's father says she is untouched," said Chiun. Baya Cayang nodded deeply.

Remo shrugged.

"Poo's father says there will never be a son."

Remo shrugged.

"Poo's father has been nice enough to keep this horrible fact from the village. The fact is, Remo, you have let us all down."

Remo rustled the scroll.

"What am I looking for?" he asked.

"I am looking for a grandson."

"And I'm looking for Mr. Arieson. The next time

I see him I want to be able to defeat him. Or is this your way of just tricking me into reading the scrolls?"

"What you want is all there. Find the treasure of Sinanju and we will be able to handle Mr. Arieson."

"Now I know you're pulling my leg. You've been trying to get that treasure back for years."

"Without it, you will never be able to handle Mr. Arieson."

"I don't want to handle him. I want to defeat him."

"Only the dead have seen the last of him," said Chiun.

"Now what does that mean?" asked Remo.

"Why have you not treated Poo properly?" asked Chiun.

"I'll get to it. I'll get to it. I'm good for it. What about this nonsense with the Greeks, and the servant to the Tyrant of Thebes?"

"Read it," said Chiun.

"I've read it. I've read it. The tribute goes on for pages."

"And?"

"And I don't understand."

"Look around you at the empty rooms. If they were not empty you would understand."

"If they were not empty this whole place would be gathering dust now with lots of junk."

"It is that junk we need now."

"I don't need it at all," said Remo.

"You need something," said Chiun. "That precious blossom awaits untouched, losing the blush of her youth while you refuse your duty to house and home, and shame us before my good friend Baya, a good and decent man who has done nothing to us but give us his treasure of a daughter."

"I'll do it. I'll do what I have to, but I don't have to

do it right away. It would help if I didn't get a runaround with these scrolls, and got some clear answers."

"You got clear answers. You were just too dim to see them," said Chiun. "There's nothing we can do about Mr. Arieson without the treasures anyhow. So enjoy the delights Poo has to offer."

"I'm not giving up," said Remo, and returned to the room Chiun had set aside for him. It was not a room for living, but one of the treasure rooms. The scrolls had been neatly laid out on a pale square piece of flooring. Something had sat on it for centuries, and the wood had become indented even though it was rare and valuable African mahogany, one of the hardest woods known to man.

The placement of the scrolls on this indentation in the floor obviously was some kind of message. But how could a place be a message? Remo rubbed his hand along the indentation in the wood. He could feel the crushed cells ever so slowly expand back from their compression, and he felt something else on his fingerpads. Dust. There was dust here in the four-foot-by-four-foot indentation.

He captured the particles in the oils of the ridges of his finger and held the dust up to the light. It was pale white. A fine white powder. No. Not powder. Marble. Something made of marble had been where the scrolls of Sinanju had been set for him.

He read the account again. It was a fairly typical service of Sinanju. A great and renowned philosopher had joined with a hero to demand an end to corruption and oppression in Thebes. The people were behind them, because the tyrant, like all basically weak people, was afraid to let anyone speak. The people had wanted to be more democratic, like Athens. They had even sent an emissary to Athens to learn their system of democracy.

No one in Thebes was on the side of the tyrant. He could not speak well, think well, or govern well, and to boot he was a coward in battle, something that offended the Greek idea of heroism. However, he did have one thing. Knowledge of the Masters of Sinanju and a willingness to pay well.

Naturally he won, and the philosopher and hero were found dead in a ravine outside the city one morning. It was said that they had dueled and the hero had desecrated the philosopher's body in a despicable way before attempting to return to Thebes, when he fell and cracked his head against a rock. Outraged, the people swarmed into the street, abandoning their loyalty to the two who were no better than murderers. Naturally it was a Sinanju service that had made the deaths seem like that.

Remo read the story again. It was followed by the usual list of tributes, and the form was the same as the rest of the House of Sinanju histories. What was strange about this story was that it was not an introduction of a new technique. The sacrilege murder had occurred first many centuries before, in the East. It was just an adaptation. But there was not even a hint of Mr. Arieson or anyone operating like him.

An old service not even new in 500 B.C., and an indentation from something marble on the floor of an empty treasure house in Sinanju.

So what?

So there was someone out there Remo couldn't get a handle on, and this wasn't telling him how.

"Master Remo. Master Remo. It's for you," came the voice. It was a young boy who had run up from the village. "The telephone in the baker's house has rung for you. Gracious Chiun has given me a piece of gold to run up here and ask you down to the house."

"He's there now?" asked Remo.

"Yes, he left the great House of Sinanju and with the baker went to see your beloved wife, Poo. They are all there with the mother. They are waiting for you, too," said the boy.

"Anyway, I can take the phone call up here."

"Master Chiun had it transferred to the baker's house so you would not be disturbed on your wedding night. No one would dare change an order from the Great Chiun."

"All right," said Remo. "I'll take it."

The call was a relay from Smith. He was all but sure Arieson was at work again in Northern Ireland. Had Remo found anything that could stop him yet?

"No," said Remo, staring at the tear-soaked moon face of Poo, the daggers of her mother's eyes, the distaste of her father, and Chiun totally siding with that family.

"Can you talk now?"

"No," said Remo.

"I think the man who calls himself Arieson is behind the kidnapping of the Prime Minister of England."

"Arieson? Where in England?"

"In Bath, obviously," said Chiun.

"Ask him how he knows it's in Bath," said Smith.

"If you take the scroll of the years of the horse, pig, and dragon, roughly your years for A.D. 112, you will not only find out why Arieson is in Bath but you will find out where in Bath."

"He's kidnapped the Prime Minister there, Little Father."

"And they can't find her, is that correct?"

"Yes. That's what they're saying. They don't know how they could have lost her," said Remo, repeating what Smith was telling him.

"They can't find her because they don't know where to look," said Chiun. "Take the scrolls with you. You'll find her. But you won't be able to stop Mr. Arieson, so don't even bother. This is where you should be bothering, with this poor, beautiful, lovely creature who wants only for you to deliver what you vowed here in your ceremony."

"I'll be right over to England, Smitty," said Remo.

Poo, he found out, had just learned another word. It was "Harrods."

8

Remo parked Poo in the Britannia Hotel in a suite of rooms overlooking one of the many little parks in London.

Before he left, she asked:

"Will you deflower me tonight?"

"If you got a petunia, I'll take it from you. But if you mean copulation, no. Not tonight."

"Why not tonight? I'm alone again on my honeymoon."

"Tonight is not the right night."

"There will never be a right night," said Poo. Somehow she had discovered, with the aid only of a phone book in a language she did not understand, that seamstresses would come up to one's hotel room and make dresses for one while one waited.

She could also order jewelers that way, too. And, of course, food. She was going to try that great English delicacy of bangers and mash.

If Poo had to be left alone again this honeymoon night, she did not know what she would tell her mother.

"Five thousand pounds," said Remo.

"I should tell my mother five thousand pounds?"

"No, you get five thousand pounds not to tell your

mother a thing about what goes on and what does not go on in our marriage."

"The first night that would be a good sum. It is not unusual for couples not to consummate the first night. It does happen. But we are into many, many nights now. Now we are beginning a disgrace." Poo's moon face quivered. A tear came down one eye. She covered her face in shame.

"How much?"

The hands lowered. "We have to be talking ten thousand pounds at least. And what is the tribute you're getting for this service?"

"I don't get the tribute. It all goes to Sinanju."

"It all goes to Chiun."

"It goes to the House of Sinanju. I am a Master of Sinanju. It goes to Chiun and me, I guess."

"I am married to a Master of Sinanju who does not even know whether he gets tribute or not. Is that what I married?"

"Divorce is possible. You can have that for a solution, Poo," said Remo, reaching the door.

"Divorce is impossible in the Sinanju ceremony. No Sinanju Master has ever gotten divorced. It isn't done. It is," said Poo, pausing before that inviolate supreme word of Sinanju, "tradition."

"There must have been one Master who got divorced. I'm sure there was," said Remo, feeling the outer edges of panic kiss his nervous system.

"You should know," cooed Poo. "You had to read all the scrolls to become a Master. If you can find a divorce in the history of Sinanju, let me know. Until then, think about how you want to divide the tribute with Chiun. It is my impression you do most of the work in the current service to America."

"How do you know that?"

"Everyone in Sinanju knows what goes on in the

House of Sinanju. It's a major topic of discussion. Am I right? Do you do most of the work?"

"We never figured out who did what, Poo. It works. There is nothing better than something that works. So long."

"But for whom does it work?" asked Poo as Remo shut the door behind him. He had to remind himself this girl was only twenty years old. What would she be like at twenty-one? What would she be like at forty, if he ever wanted to live that long?

No divorce, he thought. Because I am a Master of Sinanju, I am married to this woman forever. And yet he was sure there had to be a divorce somewhere in four thousand years. It was probably covered up. That's how those things worked.

But he had been poring over the scrolls more now than ever before, and every time a Sinanju Master was married, it was duly recorded. And every time a Sinanju wife died it was duly recorded, as was the departure of a Master. No Master ever recorded a separation. Every wife died married to a Sinanju Master, from the Great Wang to the Lesser Gi. Even Chiun's wife had died.

Poo was Remo's forever. And vice versa.

Remo arrived in Bath, in the southwest part of England, and ran into more English plainclothesmen than attended a royal wedding. It was a strange sight to see cars backed up at roadblocks for miles. Men with walkie-talkies occupied virtually every building.

Remo was spotted as someone who didn't belong there as soon as he entered Avon county, home of the town of Bath.

He brought with him only a bamboo satchel containing a Sinanju parchment.

A bobby stepped in and courteously asked him

what he was doing in these parts, and what was in the satchel.

"Something to read," said Remo. The bobby examined Remo's passport.

"You say you're visiting the mineral baths. May I ask why now?"

"Keeps me young."

"You're about twenty-eight, aren't you?"

"Would you believe you're off by at least twenty years?"

"Really?"

"Yeah. I'm eight," said Remo.

The bobby was not amused. Plainclothesmen desperately looking for something, anything, closed in on Remo. Remo had stepped out of his taxi at the roadblock and the driver was now indicating he never saw Remo before, did not know the man, and Remo was just another fare who hadn't paid yet.

"This isn't a laughing matter, Mr. Williams. Our prime minister has been kidnapped in this area, and we regret that certain precautions must be taken. These precautions may limit your freedom."

"Fine, just tell me where not to go and I won't go."

"I'm afraid, Mr. Williams, we cannot let you in this area."

"And I'm afraid, old boy, I'm just going to have to go in."

"Then I will keep your passport."

"Frame it if you will," said Remo.

"We're going to have to stop you physically."

" 'Fraid I can't let you," said Remo, and whistling, walked past the bobby in the high blue hat. Apologizing, several plainclothesmen warned they would have to stop Mr. Williams. Apologizing, Remo said he couldn't let them do that.

He whipped out the scroll and tried to get his bearings. From the center of the little resort city, he knew where he should go to look. But he had to get to the baths themselves first.

Several arms reached out for him, and he let his body respond to the air pressure ahead of the hands so he could dodge the hands while thinking about something else. It was more an absentminded gesture than a calculated move, letting the body itself do the dodging as he walked down the road reading the scroll of Master Wa, who had been hired by Emperor Claudius of Rome to make sure a plot against him did not develop within the legions occupying Roman Britain.

It was always a threat, Remo had learned from the scrolls, that some praetor would march his legions back from the frontiers and take over Rome. Caesar had done it. Others tried to do it, and this period of turmoil within the Western world, of plots and counterplots revolving around a corrupt and debauched center of authority, had proved to be what would be later called "one of the golden ages of Sinanju."

For as Master Wa wrote:

"No emperor slept nor senator spoke without fear of death in the night from the hand of an assassin. Sinanju, naturally, was the most in demand."

Remo felt an officer whiz by him as his body curved out of the way of the officer's lunge. The officer went forward on the dark country road, skinning his hands painfully.

Chiun had selected this scroll. He knew Mr. Arieson would be in Bath. Why?

Was Mr. Arieson seeking out Remo? And if so, why? Obviously Arieson and the House of Sinanju went way back. But how?

And what were the mysterious techniques Mr. Arieson used to avoid blows? Two more British policemen swung out at thin air. Did Mr. Arieson use techniques like Remo's, only more advanced?

No. Mr. Arieson would have been dodging the air currents Remo had created back at Little Big Horn if that were the case. And what about the helmet and chest protector the Israeli archaeologist said were perfectly new, punctured using a technique more than two thousand years old?

Remo hadn't even seen the helmet and chest protector. But there they were when his blows landed on metal aboard the USS *Polk*.

"Stop that man. Stop him," came a voice from behind.

"We're trying. He's made of air," answered one of the policemen.

"Then bloody well follow him," came the voice.

Remo nodded. That would be all right. They could follow him right up until he decided they might be in the way. And so Remo walked into the old Roman town of Bath, reading his scroll, certain now that Arieson was in some way taunting him. Arieson was trying to tell him something by coming to a city where Sinanju had worked. After all, hadn't Arieson phoned him, calling him "boyo"?

The answer was here in a part of England that had once belonged to Rome.

The town of Bath was pleasant, with old Tudor dwellings and modern dwellings, and what was left of Rome had been reconstructed in the mineral-water baths themselves. Bacteria had formed down at the base of the springs in the old Roman piping, which had to be removed. In the process, many coins and artifacts were found.

The baths were housed in a building, and in that

building Remo went to a section where he was supposed to get dressed, and laid out the scroll in full.

The Praetor Maximus Granicus had set up his headquarters here because he had aching bones. He had wanted to be near the springs as long as possible, until he and his legions left the Britannic shores for Gaul and Rome.

Granicus, like most ambitious men, loved luxury, and along the military road two stadia north, he built himself a palace which was supposed to be impenetrable to entry by anyone but friends.

"This Granicus domicile," the scroll went on, "had walls collapsing within walls, so that portholes were really traps. Secret entrances beneath the domicile were really mazes, and the beauty of this defensive structure was that the only way to enter it was to know how it worked.

"While I as a Master would love to record a new defense overcome by me, Wa, I regret that it was not a challenge at all, although later I would tell the Divine Claudius how dangerous it was, describing the gigantic trap as the worst obstacle of all. This, of course, was in keeping with the rule of the Great Wang, that no assassination should ever be made to look easy. A client does not think you are more wonderful because the work was easy, rather he thinks you deserve less.

"The great Granicus' defensive network was really only a weak imitation of Pharaoh Ka's lower cataract home, which was a brilliant interpretation of early-Su-dynasty imperial residences. It was penetrated easily by an open confrontation in the main, not the auxiliary entrances, which could prove problematic. Granicus was completed with a simple death during sleep, a smothering with his own pillow. His legions were given to a more loyal Claudian servant, and the civil war was averted. Tribute: pearls, three saludia in weight, eighteen in number; gold in the sum of forty-two Hibernian pharongs; twelve minor rubies, seven obols apiece; and a lengthy laudation from Claudius with an offer of games in the honor of Sinanju, offer declined."

Remo folded up the scroll. Since there was only one place mentioned in the scrolls Chiun had given him, and since Chiun knew before being told that the area where the Prime Minister had disappeared had to be Bath, therefore Remo concluded the place of action had to be the old defensive home of Granicus Maximus, two stadia north on the military road.

Since Granicus, even if he had not left the world early with the help of a Sinanju Master, would have been gone for almost two thousand years now, and since everyone who ever knew him would have been gone that long, and since anyone who knew the people who knew him would have been gone by centuries also, Remo Williams didn't bother to ask for directions but simply headed north.

In a British control base, the stranger in the gray slacks and black T-shirt was being duly recorded. It was recorded that he entered the house containing the springs, read a scroll, and then asked the nearest person, who happened to be a plainclothesman like most everyone now in this area, where the old military road was.

Constable Blake answered.

"There was a road here used to store arms for D-Day, if that's what you mean, sir."

The stranger, named Remo Williams if his passport was correct, answered:

"No. Not that one. An older one."

" 'Twas built on an old Norman road, sir," said Constable Blake.

"Bit older. How many roads north do you have?"

"Quite a few."

"What's the oldest?"

"I wouldn't rightly know, sir."

The subject, Remo, was followed to the roads north. He looked at every one of them and walked around, a bit confused. He asked several passersby how long a stadium was, and was told by a young schoolgirl the exact distance.

The schoolgirl also knew which was the old Roman road. She pointed out little white posts about a foot high along the side of the road. She told Remo:

"These are Roman mileposts. They left them all over their empire. Any idiot knows that."

"I'm an American," Remo said as Scotland Yard prepared to remove the girl from danger—if that were possible, considering the strange powers of this intruder.

"Oh, I'm sorry. Just follow the white posts. Can you count?"

"I can count. I just didn't know which was the old Roman road, that's all."

"Yes, of course. That's all right. You really can't be expected to know all these things. Just follow the white posts."

"Lots of people don't know Roman mileposts."

"Yes. Many don't. If you get lost, ask for help from a bobby," said the little girl, age nine.

"I can find it," said Remo, who could count the number of men watching him in surveillance, who could even sense the monitors on him sending signals back to their headquarters.

"I'm sure you can," said the sweet little girl with the separate teeth, schoolbooks, freckles, braids, and all the other usual accoutrements of an English schoolchild. "Just don't walk in the middle of the road, sir. Cars are dangerous."

Remo cleared his throat. "Cars are not dangerous. I'm dangerous."

"Well of course you're dangerous. You're a very dangerous man," she said, humoring him the way children sometimes do with adults. "But please do stay on the side of the road."

Remo saw a police van parked along the side of the road. It was the one containing the cameras watching him.

He sauntered over to one headlight and unscrewed it. Along with the tires, the man at the wheel, the wheel, and finally with a great roaring rip, the roof.

"Dangerous," said Remo.

"Destructive," said the British schoolgirl.

The Scotland Yard detectives poured out of the van without a roof.

"Stay where you are. I'm going to get you your prime minister. Just don't crowd me."

"Do stay near him," said the girl. "He can be violent, of course, but he does seem like a dear sort, don't you think?"

"I'm not a dear sort," said Remo. "I'm an assassin. I kill people. I kill lots of people."

"Well then, they must be nasty people, but do please stay on the side of the road, and do be careful whom you let offer you a ride."

Remo shot the onlooking police a dirty glance. He could hear one of them say into a telphone:

"Subject identified self as dangerous assassin."

Remo blew a raspberry at the police, and one at the little girl, and counted his way up the old Roman road for as many white posts as the girl said.

He knew the road had to be underneath him.

That was how roads worked. They built new roads on top of old roads, and they just layered the pathways. Or wore them down as the case might be. It was the same thing they did with cities. They just kept piling the new city on top of the old one.

Remo reached the correct milepost and looked around. To his right was a field of grain. To his left was a flock of sheep. Stone walls surrounded the road, and far off was a little cottage billowing smoke.

There was no ruin of a mansion. Not a hint of an old Roman building. Nothing. British countryside and nothing.

"He's stopped just where they left the Prime Minister's car. He's looking around," came a voice that was supposed not to carry as far as Remo could hear.

"He's turning around now, looking back here, putting a finger over his mouth. By Jove, the man can hear me a half-mile away down the road."

If Remo could not get quiet, he would have to make it around him. A thrush called at a distance, idling motors chugged far off, wind blew through the grain, and Remo inhaled, tasting first the odors of the earth, moisture, rich soil, old gasoline fumes, and then from skin to bone he became quiet in himself, selecting the sounds and noises and scents and closing them off one by one until he was in a silence of his body.

He could taste the harsh macadam road through his shoes. There was stone under that road, deep and heavy stone. The earth was interrupted by it. A half-mile off was a little grassy hillock.

Remo remembered Chiun pointing out an old building in Judea once. He said when buildings were in countrysides, if the site was not maintained, it would grow over. And if it grew over for more than a few centuries, the plants and earth would build a small hill around it. Only recently in modern times had archaeololgists learned to recognize these hills as tels, good digging sites for old cities and such.

Remo walked over the stone wall and through the field of golden grain to the green hillock. He stood there and knew there was lots of stone underneath. He walked wherever he felt stone until he saw where the earth had been cut. Usually grass was hacked away, but this cut was done with something as smooth as a scalpel cutting a line the length of a coffin low in the hill. It was a patch, a patch of earth cut and replaced and now beginning to grow back.

Remo dug into it with his hands and peeled it back. He heard the constables back at the road say he had found something. He saw loose dirt underneath. Someone had recently dug here, and it was easy to follow. It took him only a few minutes to reach the first minor stone baffle in the outer wall of the old home of Maximus Granicus, sent early to his reward by the hand of Sinanju.

Hazel Thurston was tired of threatening that her captors would never get away with this. Besides, she didn't believe it anymore herself.

They *were* going to get away with it. They had kidnapped her just outside Bath in the quintessentially British county of Avon, and they had gotten clean away with it. They hadn't left the country, and yet she was in a strange stone room with earth piled up outside the windows.

They had been here three days now, and the water was tepid, the food old, and as she suspected, the air was getting stale.

"Do you think they buried us without air?" asked the intelligence aide.

"Must be a big place if we could last until now."

"Looks like we're lost, yes?" said the aide.

"I'm afraid so."

"What do you say we overpower the guard?"

"Certainly. But what for? Where are we going to run?"

"We can start digging."

"We don't know how much earth they piled up outside."

"I can hear you," said the guard. He held a submachine gun loosely at his side.

"Then you should know you're going to get nothing from me."

"I wouldn't want anything from you, Hazel Thurston," said the guard. "You're an ugly old Brit bitch to begin with."

"In victory or defeat, you people are just as disgusting as the day your mothers foaled you," said the British Prime Minister. The aide shot her a look of caution.

"What are you afraid of?" she asked. "That he won't like us?"

"If I didn't like you, bitch, you'd have your eyes shot out."

"I am sure that is the new form of government you wish to bring to Ireland. I don't know why people are surprised that when terrorist movements take over a country, they just use the police force the way they use you louts."

The courageous woman's chest heaved. The air was getting very thin. The guard had a little plastic tube he sucked on every few minutes. He was getting fresh oxygen.

"If I am going to pass out," said Hazel Thurston, "I do have a last word. Please get your leader here."

"You can tell it to me."

"I wouldn't leave my used tissues with you. Get your leader."

Mr. Arieson arrived without one of those tubes that apparently supplied oxygen. He didn't seem to need air. He was fresh as sunshine.

"You want to see me? You have a last word?"

"Yes, I do. I feel myself on the verge of passing out. And I want you to be aware of my last sentiments."

"I love last sentiments," said Mr. Arieson. "I love monuments to last sentiments. I love banners with last sentiments, and standards with last sentiments, and a statue with a last heroic sentiment absolutely makes me swoon."

"God save the Queen, and God save England," said the Prime Minister, and was feeling a darkness envelop her when one of the walls caved in, sending a large block of stone smashing into the room as though it had been shot from a cannon.

A man followed it inside. Blessed air filled the room. It became light. The terrorist with the submachine gun brought it to bear. He was a large man with thick forearms. The intruder, smaller and thinner, seemed to just slap at the forearms. But it sounded like thunder. The arms looked like jelly in the sleeves, and the submachine gun fell harmlessly to the ground.

The man caved in the terrorist's head like an inflated paper bag.

The intelligence man gasped. "I've never seen moves that fast or effective. Ever. That's not a man. I don't know what it is."

"He's from an old house I know," said Arieson, who didn't bother to hide or duck.

"You. I want you," said Remo.

"Here I am," said Arieson. "I obviously wanted you. And here you are. Don't you get the message yet?"

"I'm waiting."

'Stay out of my way."

"You set things up for me to be here and you say I'm in your way."

"You people are always in my way. I try to have a little fun, do my thing, and you always cause trouble. Sinanju are the biggest troublemakers of all time. Look here at this old unused house of Granicus Maximus, who by the way knew how to treat me, if you don't. You killed him before he had his civil war."

"Who are you?" asked Hazel Thurston.

"I'm someone who doesn't like to be interfered with," said Mr. Arieson.

"I'm your rescuer," said Remo to the Prime Minister. "Or didn't you mean me?"

"I meant both of you. Get out of my way, please."

"Just a second," said Remo. "I'm going to try to kill this guy."

"Be our guest, but please do let me out first," said the Prime Minister. She saw Scotland Yard types at the entrance to the room the thin stranger had made. She told them to wait.

The thin stranger picked up a block of stone from the floor that must have weighed a ton. He did it in a gentle motion, and then the stone was chest-high and then it was flying through the air at Arieson. But the stranger was moving alongside it, as though waiting for Arieson to duck. He did not duck. He walked through the stone, and through the wall, calling out:

"Salve gladiati."

The stone shattered like shrapnel, wounding the Prime Minister lightly on her forearm and cutting a small gash in her aide's head. The thin stranger left a little less mysteriously. Whereas Arieson appeared to move through solid stone, the thin stranger moved through solid phalanx of Scotland Yard.

He was lost by the police on the road back to Bath, but later the Prime Minister found out in a confidential phone call from America's President that the stranger was American and had been sent to rescue Prime Minister Thurston.

"He seems to have amazing moves," said the Prime Minister. "But who is this Arieson and what terror group does he represent?"

"We don't know yet."

"Well, it certainly can function better than any of the hostiles before it."

"That's what worries us," said the President. He did not tell his ally, but Harold W. Smith of CURE had set up a strategy room just for this phenomenon. It tracked all the methods of the new warfare and found that previously ineffective groups had suddenly developed not only a skill for warfare but also a desire for it, something that the military academies could only hope to instill. Something was making men want to go to war more than had ever been recorded in the insane history of the planet.

Remo arrived back in Sinanju with Poo, and his puzzle. While he could do nothing with Arieson, he had a plan for Poo. He brought her to live in the big house on the hill, as was befitting the wife of a Master of Sinanju.

There he asked Chiun to speak with her.

"As an American I want my wife to be part of our business," said Remo.

"Most foolish, like most things American."

"Poo's got some good ideas about how to run the House of Sinanju."

"Really?" said Chiun. He folded his long fingernails in his lap and his face was calm.

"Yeah, she thinks we ought to formalize our relationship. You know, who gets what for what. Right now it goes into one big kitty. I don't keep track of it. But I'd like you to talk to her."

Remo said this with a straight face. And with just as straight a face, Chiun said he would be delighted.

He allowed Poo to make a place for herself on a mat before him. She served them tea. Chiun's was little more than warm water. Hers was harsh and black. Remo sat down between them with the countenance of an innocent.

Poo began with praises for the Masters of Sinanju, and then began recounting tales of their wives. Remo had never heard these stories before.

Poo seemed to know just from stories handed down what each wife got, and how she was treated. Chiun only nodded. He did not disagree with anything she said. When she was finished it was past midnight and the dank West Korea Bay was dark as a buried slate.

"Are you done with your demands?" asked Chiun.

"I am, dear father-in-law."

"Then may I wish you luck with Remo, because he is the only one to negotiate, for it is his share that is yours, not mine. And as between Remo and me, we've already arranged things."

"But what share does Remo get?"

"Whatever share I say he gets. That is the tradition of Sinanju."

Remo saw blood drain from the round face of Poo.

"Look, sweetheart," he said, "if you feel tricked into this marriage, you can back out now."

"No," she wailed. "No Master of Sinanju ever gets divorced."

Chiun smiled, leaving Remo with Poo, who now wanted a better accounting of Remo's property than an American CPA. Just before he was out of sight, Chiun said:

"The next time Mr. Arieson calls, and he will, I will go with you. And I'll show you how to handle him."

9

"Does Chiun know him?"

"I think so," said Remo. He was on the line with Smith in the baker's house. The baker's wife had a new dress from Harrods. As she prepared the evening dinner, she passed by Remo, making gestures. There would be a finger turned limply downward, and a contemptuous smile. There would be a noodle draped over a bowl and then a pointing to Remo. An old man would walk outside, stooped over, and she would nod to the old man while smiling to Remo, indicating the same performance could be expected from Remo.

Remo ignored her. In all the world, he had never gotten so much disrespect as in Sinanju itself. Especially from Poo's family. He could probably change it, but that would require making love to Poo. He would sooner dip his body in braised chicken liver with raw onions. He would rather swim nude through warm aspic. He would mount a vat of frozen marmalade first.

These were the things he thought of precious Poo, and the more he thought them, the more he did not wish to make love to this woman, not once. Not quickly like a chipmunk. Not ever.

It was not that Poo was fat. Weight on a nice woman could be attractive. Poo was at the core, if one could wade through to the core, a very un-nice person. She was like a magnet for every personality flaw of womankind.

Three minutes in the King David Hotel and Poo had adopted the spending habits of a Great Neck, Long Island, matron.

She came back from London like the worst of British royalty, thinking everyone around her had to be either condescended to or ignored.

She wanted to become his business partner.

And she used her mother like her own personal whip. Remo could feel for the baker, a truly harried man. In a society where women were supposed to be subservient, he was like a slave.

The fact was, for some reason the attitude of even the nicer Sinanju women was that a man was only good for what he could do for her. Remo had never heard really kind words from Chiun about his wife, other than that he had managed to live with her. But then the Masters of Sinanju had something else. They had Sinanju. That was more than a wife or a mistress: it was the one permanent relationship a Master would have. Everything else passed.

There was a closeness Remo, born in Newark in America, had with Chiun and every other Master for millennia that transcended anything humans shared with each other. It was a knowing. It was a being. Even if he and Chiun were at diametrically opposite positions on any matter, they were, after all, the same. More the same than twins. So as Remo tried to explain to Smith what the situation was, in a way he couldn't.

"He recognized Arieson. From the beginning. At Little Big Horn."

"Who is he?"

"It's not something he can tell me," said Remo.

"Why not? Look, I don't know if you realize what we're up against. But here is a person, a movement, a thing if you will, that cannot be stopped."

"I stopped him."

"No you didn't, Remo," said Smith. They had gone over all three incidents in detail, with Smith asking his usual calculated questions. And they had gone over them again and again. And each time, Smith became more worried.

"What we have here, Remo, and I have analyzed this thoroughly, is a person or system or something that cannot be stopped. The evidence so far indicates he has stopped of his own free will, not because you did anything."

"Physically, I can't stop him yet. The answer may be in the Sinanju scrolls."

"I'm not sure what answer you'll find. Are you aware of what truly worries your president and me?"

Remo turned away from the baker's wife and faced out into the street. It was noon and the sun baked the cold slate waters of the West Korea Bay. Gulls dipped and winged, and landed on rocks and fishing boats, cawing insolently to the muddy little village.

"There seems to be no rational motive behind what he is doing. It's like a rocket going every which way. The man has no purpose anyone can divine. First he helps the Indians in a war, then he turns the Idrans into soldiers attacking a U.S. aircraft carrier. Then he takes random units of the Irish Republican Army and turns them into one of the finest fighting units ever to wage war in Europe. Then he leaves, and everything he has built falls apart and he starts again. What is this person or thing up to?"

"He seems to have an old feud with the House of Sinanju. At least Chiun recognized him."

"All right. You know Sinanju, Remo. How many feuds has Sinanju had?"

"We don't. That's just it. Nowhere in the scrolls does it say we have a feud anywhere. But look, don't worry."

"Why not?"

"Chiun told me he'll show me how to deal with him."

"I hope he's right, Remo. This morning someone kidnapped the pope. The Italian police, who cannot enter the Vatican, report that for the first time in centuries the Swiss Guards are ready to fight a war."

"Good. Sounds like Mr. Arieson. Now we'll let Chiun show me how to handle this."

For Rome, Chiun packed a black kimono with silver embroidery, a gift from the finest Italian family to the House of Sinanju several centuries before.

There was a florid parchment in the folds which read:

"To a house we have learned to appreciate—your good and faithful friends the Borgias."

"We haven't used this kimono since we worked in Italy," said Chiun on the small hovercraft taking them to the waiting aircraft carrier where they would pick up their military flight to Rome. "A good family, the Borgias. Except they suffered from a do-it-yourself complex. They couldn't leave well enough alone. Lucretia Borgia used poison, and because she thought that the goodness of an assassination lay only in killing someone, the whole family ended up with a bad reputation in history. How many times have we seen a successful ruling family fall because they can't leave well enough alone? So many think they can do it themselves just because we make it look easy."

"What are you going to do with Arieson?" asked Remo.

"You'll see," said Chiun.

"I'd feel a lot better if I knew."

"I'd feel a lot better if you knew, too. But you don't, do you?"

Before they went to the Vatican, Chiun insisted on walking the streets of Rome. Some of the ancient marblework had been preserved, the old forum looking like a partial skeleton of marble, withered in the adjacent modern street. They passed the old home of the Vestal Virgins, pagan priestesses, on whose example modern convent life in the Catholic Church was modeled. And then, of course, the bitter little remnants of the old temples to the old gods that were no more.

Before Christianity there were only these gods in what was called the civilized world. For every attribute—love, drinking, war, the sea—there was a special god. From Venus to Neptune these gods ruled the daily lives of the people and received their offerings.

But with the advent of Christianity, with the promise of eternal life, with a god who had died for his people, an unseen God from the Hebrews, the great temples became empty, and the last priests lived alone without followers, without offerings, tending the statues of their cults.

And when the priests were gone, when the coffers built up over hundreds and hundreds of years were finally empty, either Christians set up their churches in these pagan temples, or as Remo saw now, the buildings just decayed. Standing before the site of the Great Temple of Jupiter, where once thousands would crowd in for feasts, Remo saw just a worn simple marble slab in the dirt of Rome with a bronze inscription saying there had been a huge temple here.

"They were good cults," said Chiun. "You knew where they stood. It was clean. You gave a god something, he gave you something back. None of this suffering for love, and an affliction as some kind of reward. We never thought Christianity would catch on, but see, here we are, and it has."

"I was raised by nuns in an orphanage. I'm going to feel funny in the Vatican."

"Don't. Remember, the Borgias were once popes and we have worked there. Ah, Rome, who would have thought you would last so long," said Chiun, waving a hand at the city on the Tiber which had once ruled the world, and now was only bad traffic and picturesque marble remnants. And of course, the Vatican, the great Vatican, where once a fighting arena had stood.

Outside the large columns, Italian police and soldiers had sealed off the entire state-within-a-state. From St. Peter's, little groups of men could be seen hacking away at each other. Some wore striped pantaloons and velvet hats. They were the Swiss Guards, who protected the post. Once they had actually fought other little armies, but now they were only ceremonial.

Until, as Remo found out, the morning when they threw over their papal banners, shouted to hell with peace, and engaged in hand-to-hand combat with a group of Turks brought in by a strange man with a muscled neck whose eyes seemed to glow.

This they learned from the carabinieri, who warned Remo and Chiun not to enter.

"It's terrible, terrible what's happening in that holy site," said the carabinieri. "But we cannot enter."

"Why not?" asked Remo.

"The Vatican is another state. Someone has to invite us in. We have not been invited. And no one will do anything in there until the pope is free."

"Is he a prisoner?"

"We think so," said the carabinieri.

A head went rolling along St. Peter's courtyard, lopped off by a Turkish scimitar.

"Horrible," said Chiun.

The carabinieri covered his eyes. "Horrible," he agreed.

"Yes, amateurs making a mess of things. Well, that's to be expected with what's let loose. Come, Remo. This is not the way to enter the Vatican. You can just tell Mr. Arieson is inside. Look at that enthusiasm for a bad stroke."

The way to enter the Vatican was the way Augustus Caesar would enter the arena. Through tunnels, protected from his citizens in case they rioted. These tunnels later became part of the catacombs of Rome.

The catacomb Remo and Chiun wanted was underneath a restaurant. Chiun calculated where the entrance used to be according to his old lessons, to which, he stressed, he devoted himself as a child, unlike Remo, and sent a fingernail into old plaster. Vibrating it within the rhythms of the molecules, he collapsed the entire wall, to the despairing shouts of the restaurant owner, who had stored olives and garlic and fresh tomatoes down there in the basement. They were all ruined now.

"We're in service of the pope," said Chiun. "Send your bill to the Vatican."

Before them rising out of the rubble was a high entrance, larger than most modern doors. On either side of this entrance were frescoes of gods and

goddesses making love, playing, and dancing. Remo
noticed the clothes on the gods were quite skimpy.

Chiun led the way, explaining the tale of the artist
who painted these frescoes. In the palace of Augustus Caesar nearby, people were being killed. Everyone thought it was Augustus' wife, Livia, again with
that great Italian attraction to poison. Actually, it was
a minor assassin employing the artist as a conduit to
the cooks.

The assassin knew the artist could buy his freedom, and was in love with another slave whose freedom he wished to buy also. So he used the artist for
access to the palace. The House of Sinanju came
along in the employ of Augustus, discovered the
plot, eliminated the competition with ease, and
brought the artist before Augustus.

Augustus, a wise ruler, understood the artist was
only a slave, expected to be weak, and let him live.
But the cook, a free man, he had crucified because
more was expected of a free man than a slave.

"It is a beautiful little story," said Chiun.

"What's beautiful about a crucifixion?" asked Remo.
The tunnels had a strange glaze from the underearth
about them. It made Remo's skin crawl.

Remo saw an old-style fresco with fine color tones
but crude lines. It reminded him of one room of the
treasures of Sinanju. He had seen that room on his
first visit to Sinanju. There were statues and jewels
and gold, and then Remo remembered, it was the
room that had the indentation in the mahogany floor.
He tried to remember what had made that indentation. But he couldn't. When one has taken on four
thousand years of accumulated treasure in one afternoon, everything tends to blur. Besides, never having received tribute, he didn't care about it too much.

They walked three miles under the Vatican and

then Chiun turned into a doorway with stone steps leading steeply upward. Above them they could hear laughter, and screams and cries and the clashing of swords.

"Disgraceful," said Chiun. "But you have to expect this now."

They pushed through a wood-and-steel door at the top of the steps opening into a vast room where tapestries hung from the walls. Ornate furniture was placed a few feet from the walls and nothing stood in the center of the room where the inlaid pink and gold marble floor was covered now by the slime of blood.

Swiss Guards swung their halberds in wide, deadly arcs against a group of Turks fighting with scimitars. Sometimes a big-bladed halberd would strike clean and a head would go rolling, or an arm would be neatly severed. More often than not it missed, striking only a glancing blow, spilling more blood. The scimitar, less useful for arm-length fighting than the long-poled halberd, was very effective at close range. It could disembowel the guards right through their velvet blouses.

In the middle of this butchery Mr. Arieson sat, a big smile on his face, rubbing his hands.

"I love it. I love it," he said. And seeing Remo and Chiun, added: "Welcome to the selfish bastards of Sinanju. See what you'd like to deprive your fellowman of? I hate you bastards, always have."

"Okay, deal with him," said Remo.

"Not now. We've got to save the pope," said Chiun.

"Since when are you a Catholic?"

"We have a sacred and binding obligation to the chair of St. Peter," said Chiun. "We have promised the Borgias."

"Good folks, the Borgias," said Mr. Arieson.

"Sometimes," said Chiun. "And never when you liked them," and pointing to Arieson Chiun told Remo: "That is a killer. Now you know the difference between a killer and a true assassin."

Remo wanted to take one last try at Arieson's stomach, just on the chance that a blow would work this time, but Chiun pulled him along.

"Is he from some other house of assassins, Little Father?"

"Him? From another house? He has no respect for assassins."

"Could you just tell me who he is, instead of beating around the bush?"

"No. You don't deserve to know."

"Well, I don't care who he is. Just show me how to deal with him when this is done."

His Holiness was being held by a group of dark young men wearing fezzes with bright crescents on them. They called themselves the new Janissaries of Turkey.

There were twenty of them around the pope, parading their new power. His Holiness sat quietly in dignity made more awesome by the fact of the noise and threats from the Turks.

"We are the new Janissaries, and we are here to revenge the insult to our glorious fighters from battles past. We are here to revenge Mehmet Ali Agha, who stood his hand for us and our glory. In other words, pontiff, we will not miss this time."

The words were spoken by the leader of the group as Remo and Chiun entered the small audience room where the pope now sat chained to a little dark wooden throne.

'We never had much use for the old Janissaries," said Chiun. "Your Holiness, we are here. Glory to the Borgias, glory to their papacy, the House of Sinanju is here to honor its pledge."

The pope, who had suffered through the nightmare of seeing his own normally docile Swiss Guards become raving maniacs, delighted at the prospect of battle with the attacking Turks, now saw an aged Oriental in a black kimono with silver embroidery and a thin white man in black T-shirt and gray trousers begin playing with the Turks.

It was like a formal dance. A Turk would swing a scimitar and follow it into a wall, yet the elderly Oriental hardly moved. The white would skewer three men on their own swords and neatly lay them in a corner.

It did not look like a battle so much as two chambermaids cleaning up a room, picking up bodies, laying them down. The younger one seemed to do more of the stacking, complaining in English that he was always the one who had to do this chore. The older one seemed to make flourishes of his kimono for the pope's pleasure.

Finally the older one severed the steel chain on the pope's wrist as though it were tissue paper and bowed low. The younger one looked shocked at this.

In a great and courtly bow, Chiun, the Master of Sinanju, kissed the pope's ring.

Remo, the Catholic orphan from Newark raised by nuns, stood with his mouth open.

"Your Holiness, we are here," said Chiun. His wisps of hair touched the floor as he reached the nadir of his bow, and then, using his kimono like wings, flourished it gloriously and stood up.

"Who are you?" asked His Holiness in English.

"A fulfiller of the wisest arrangement ever made by the throne of St. Peter."

"Would you tell me the arrangement? This has

been a most trying day." The white still stood with
his mouth open, looking at the pope's ring.

To Remo, an ex-Catholic who had never heard a
Christian word from Chiun, this ornate sign of per-
fect obedience seemed to him as strange as a talking
flounder. He couldn't believe it. But he had seen it.
It was better than in St. Monica's back in Newark.
The nuns could not have improved one whit on the
way Chiun, the Master of Sinanju, had greeted His
Holiness. It wasn't that Chiun even kissed the ring.
It was the hearty way he went at it. Remo would
have thought Chiun had just entered the priesthood.

"Your Holiness, the accords between the Vatican
and the House of Sinanju were established during
the magnificent pontificate of the Borgia popes."

The pope tilted his strong and kindly face.

"Sir," he said. "One of the proofs of the divine
inspiration of the Catholic Church is that we survived the likes of the Borgia popes. We survived and
triumphed over that decadence and murder. We
have been reaffirmed by His hand against our sins."

"We have only fond memories of the Borgia popes."

"I do not understand who you are."

"We are the House of Sinanju, assassins to the
finest of the world."

The pope shook his head. "I want no accords with
assassins," he said, and asked the date the supposed
document had been drawn. Once given the date, he
sent for an aide, and the aide sent for another aide,
and that aide sent for a nun who found the parchment, sealed with the three-tiered crown of St. Peter.

The pontiff read the document with wide eyes.
The Borgias, that disgrace to the Catholic Church,
had purchased the services of these Oriental assassins in perpetuity; for a set fee the House of Sinanju
agreed never to serve an enemy of the pope.

"No," said His Holiness. "We will not have this. You are free of your pledge."

"Your Holiness, we have adopted some most Christian customs in honor of your saintliness. Like marriage," said Chiun. "We Masters do not believe in divorce. Marriage is a bond not to be broken. Remo, my son, raised a Catholic, seems not to understand this."

The pope looked at his attackers, now stacked against the wall. In truth, these two had saved him. He asked the white man what should be so complicated about the marriage vow.

"Fulfilling it," said Remo. He did not bow down to kiss the ring, any more than he would talk in flowery nonsense to Harold W. Smith.

"One owes certain duties to one's spouse."

"I know. But I didn't want to marry her in the first place. Not really. I only did it to get my father, Chiun, to help me figure something out, something that had to do with that maniac Arieson."

"Then you did not enter this union of your own free will, my son?"

"No, Holy Father," said Remo.

"And Sinanju's customs regarding marriage are the same as those of the Holy Roman Catholic Church?"

"They are, Holy Father," said Remo.

"Then the marriage never took place. Only when someone enters a marriage freely and then consummates it is it a true marriage."

"I certainly haven't consummated that thing," said Remo.

"Then your marriage definitely does not exist, for two reasons."

Remo jumped almost to the ceiling, then fell on his knees and with awesome gratitude kissed the ring of the pope even though he didn't believe anymore. He would have kissed the hem of this man's garment. He was free of Precious Poo. The marriage did not exist.

"I'm free, Little Father, isn't that wonderful?" said Remo.

Chiun, kissing the pope's ring with just as grand a flourish, muttered in Korean about the perfidy of Rome.

Arieson was still in the large room with the tapestries, waiting for Remo and Chiun.

"I hear you rescued your client, Chiun," said Arieson.

"I have come to deal with you, Arieson," said Chiun, folding his arms and setting one foot forward in a posture of supreme arrogant bearing.

"Sure, Chiun. What's the deal?" said Arieson, leaning back in the chair and sending encouragement to the last Turk to fight to the death.

"We will stay out of Western Europe if you stay out of Asia," said Chiun.

"I'm not giving up China and Japan. I've enjoyed those places immensely," said Arieson.

"Japan is worthless now. It manufactures toys. What do you want with Japan?"

"That's only in the last fifty years. You don't think they've changed totally in the last fifty years? I can't let you have Japan."

"How many good markets are there?" asked Chiun. "Look at what I'm walking away from. America. Now, that's an active country for you. South America. It's coming into its age, and all of Europe, and the Middle East. Do you wish to deal or not?"

"You're not in a position to bargain. You can't give me what I want or deserve. You just don't have the goods anymore. You can cause me a little trouble here and there, but your boy Remo is just a diversion. I will let you have Japan."

"And Indochina."

"No. Too much."

"You have all China. You have Russia. Are we bargaining or are you dictating?" asked Chiun.

"Done," said Arieson. He offered a hand that Chiun refused to shake.

"Done," said Chiun.

Arieson offered the same hand to Remo.

"No," said Remo. "No deals. And you, Little Father, you said you'd show me how to deal with Arieson."

"I just did. We just did. You don't want to live with it, that's all."

"Walking away from most of the world, Little Father, is not dealing with Mr. Arieson."

"It's the best I can do until you get back the treasure of Sinanju."

"That's still lost, is it?" laughed Arieson.

"How do you know so much?" asked Remo.

"I just watch you guys hack around and laugh my insides out," said Areison. "Let me tell you about this city. It's good to be home again. I hated Hibernia, and your new country, Remo."

"What the hell do you want?" asked Remo.

"To do what I do. I'll get what I want unless you fellas give me what I deserve."

"And what does that mean?" asked Remo.

"Chiun will tell you. Don't worry, only the dead have seen the last of me."

"Well, you haven't seen the last of me," said Remo.

"Wanta fight, big boy?" laughed Arieson.

This time Remo tried something entirely strange. If all the blows of Sinanju had not worked, then perhaps a straight punch to the stomach, fairly slow, not much faster than a professional boxer, would work. Remo let it go and shattered the fine wooden chair on which Mr. Arieson had sat.

The room was filled with the dead and the quiet. But not with Mr. Arieson.

"I can believe this troublemaker has some strange powers. But I can't believe, Little Father, that pile of junk you call the treasure of Sinanju has any bearing on this. You just want it back."

"Until we regain the treasure of Sinanju, Remo, we will be helpless against Mr. Arieson. I am sorry you do not believe me. But you can believe this. Until we regain that treasure, I will consider you obliged to consummate your marriage with Poo."

"But you heard the pope. I'm not married. I've never been married."

"That's for Roman Catholics, Remo. You're Sinanju."

"But you said you followed the Catholic laws."

"And since when, Remo, do you believe anything I tell an emperor?" said Chiun.

They left the Vatican the way they came. Out on the street in front of the restaurant, where the owner was trying to have the two arrested for ruining his basement, Chiun said:

"We have missed the glorious ages of Sinanju, Remo. Make a son for us, so that he might see an age of assassinry, where the corrupt and despotic do not take their people to war, but hire professionals like ourselves to do the proper work."

"I'm happy with the time I'm in," said Remo.

"You're never happy," said Chiun.

"Neither are you," said Remo.

"No," said Chiun, "I always say I am unhappy but I enjoy it. You always say you are happy but you never enjoy it."

"I'm not going back to Sinanju, Little Father."

"And I am not leaving Sinanju until you recover the treasure."

"Then good-bye, Little Father," said Remo.

"Good-bye," said Chiun, refusing to look at him.

"Would you want to marry Poo if you were me?" asked Remo. But Chiun did not answer. He chose to walk around one of his favorite cities as Remo hailed a cab to take him to the airport.

Back in America, Smith made the rare gesture of allowing Remo to return to Folcroft, an area he was supposed to avoid to help sustain the cover of the sanitarium. Remo as well as Chiun had been seen at random points around the country, but no one had yet connected them to the organization housed on Long Island Sound. No one, that is, who was allowed to live.

Smith was even more serious as he brought Remo into a special situation room, with maps on the wall and grids on a table. They were alone here, and Remo could see that Smith was figuring out patterns of Mr. Arieson.

"So far, Mr. Arieson has been random, like a ball in a roulette wheel. He would bounce into a major area of conflict and bounce to a minor one."

Remo nodded this was true.

"Now, he is back to the most major of all. I think we're going to have a war with Soviet Russia, and you may be the only one who can stop it," said Smith.

"Stop it?" asked Remo. "I can't even lay a hand on the guy." But even now, he was having an especially good thought about Russia, and her name was Anna.

10

Anna Chutesov once again saw the panic. It always came with field marshal's braid on its shoulders, and the traditional ranking officer's field cap.

Panic came in stone faces talking with apparent calm about opportunities and risks. It always came cloaked in that all-encompassing garbage bag called:

"National Security."

In Russia those words were more holy and central to life than Jesus was to Christianity. And they were always invoked when the military leadership was being pressured to act rationally in a time of crisis.

"Comrade Sister Chutesov, you cannot call in the Americans. You are endangering national security," said a field marshal who had survived the Second World War and Stalin and had enough big shiny medals on his chest to fill a checkerboard. He was indeed a hero of the Soviet Union, known for his implacable calm in the face of danger.

All heads nodded around the little clearing in the woods just south of Moscow. There were fifteen generals and Politburo members. Their most loyal aides, some colonels, some majors, stood just beyond the clearing with AK-47's at the ready. Some of the men stamped their feet to keep out the early-autumn cold. Someone passed around a lone hot cup of tea.

Anna ignored the cold. She always wore the latest thermal underclothes from the West as soon as September came and switched to lighter clothes only in the middle of April.

Her head was bundled in a fur hat and her fine beautiful high-cheekboned features were framed by a band of silvery fur. If anything, this strategic adviser to the Premier looked like a Kewpie doll. She spoke in a low whisper that forced the taller men to lean down to hear her.

"And you think national security has not been breached? What, then, is the top military command doing meeting here like frightened rabbits in a hole?"

"But to willfully invite an American operative into the inner reaches of our command structure. To invite a foreigner here to attack Russians. It is treason." This from the commander of the KGB, a field marshal in a stiff green uniform.

"Tell me, field marshal, what would you propose instead? The fact is, you are supposed to run the finest security network in the world. The fact is, comrade field marshal, you are helpless."

"If the Premier—"

"The Premier is not here. Most of your junior officers are not here. We do not know which units of the KGB are with the government and which are not. We do not know which units of the great Red Army are with us or not. We do not know which units of the air force and the navy are with us or not. We know one thing: major elements of our defensive structure have suddenly gone berserk. We cannot control them and the government is terrified that we are definitely heading into a major war with America."

"Well, that's our problem," said the KGB commander. His name was Nevsky. He had a face like a beagle's. It looked kind. But the man wasn't. He made a motion with his hands indicating the case was closed.

"It's our problem," said Anna. "And there is nothing anyone of us here can do about it. We are meeting here in these woods instead of the Kremlin precisely because none of us knows which of his own units will kidnap him the way our premier has been kidnapped. We are here because we cannot solve the problem."

"But they are our units," said the army field marshal. "They are Russian. They have, like many of us, become frustrated by this long twilight war orchestrated by the KGB as the way to defeat the West. They are tired of getting new tanks and seeing them rust as they become outmoded before being used in combat. The soldiers of the brave Red Army are better than watchdogs on our border. They are warriors."

'I see you too have been infected by that mysteriously sudden disease that has spread throughout the defense forces."

"Honor and courage are not a disease," said the army field marshal. His name was Rossocov. When he spoke, his pantheon of medals jingled.

"When the army decides it is going to declare war on America itself, and kidnaps the Premier to do so, I would say that is a bit of a trauma in the body of the defense system," said Anna. "The arms and legs have gone off without the head. And the head stands around here in these woods, terrified of getting its body back."

"The army might win. You don't know it will lose," said Field Marshal Rossocov.

KGB Field Marshal Nevsky nodded agreement. A few of the Politburo also nodded. Even if this was a Russian rebellion, it was still being run by Russian communists.

It was then that Anna Chutesov stepped into the center of the little circle in the cleared section of the woods. She inhaled the cold Russian autumn air and said more loudly than she had before, loudly but not quite a scream:

"Win what?"

Then she turned and looked every one of them in the eye.

Finally Field Marshal Rossocov said bluntly:

"The war."

"And what does the war win us?" she asked.

"Victory," said Rossocov.

"What is the gain of that victory, which, by the way, could well result in the annihilation of multi-millions and a planet much less inhabitable than before?"

"The gain is that we have destroyed the center of capitalism. We have defeated our major foe. We have triumphed against the strongest nation in the world."

"You still didn't answer the question," said Anna.

Rossocov wanted to slap the woman across her pretty face. Women could never understand war like men, even the brilliant Anna Chutesov.

"Defeating capitalism is not winning something."

"It most certainly is. It is the triumph of communism. It is the end of the struggle. No more war."

"Excuse me, but this flies in the face of reality. We have until recently been closer to war with China, a communist country, than with America. So the triumph of international communism as we know it will not mean an end to war any more than the advent of Christianity among nations meant an end to war."

"Is the triumph of communism nothing, then?" asked Field Marshal Rossocov.

Anna could see the sympathy for this argument in the faces around her, supported by the patriotic and socialist fervor they had lived with all their lives.

Men she thought. What idiots. She wanted to say, "Probably nothing," but that would have required in these men a sophistication to understand that every social system tended to function by its own human rules rather than the ones laid down from the top, like communism.

Instead, she stressed again that the defeat of capitalism would not mean an end to struggle, that there would always be more enemies and that they would face those enemies on a planet far less inhabitable than it was before.

"Given that there is no prospect of winning anything worthwhile, and given that we cannot do anything about this mental disease infecting vast segments of the Russian defense forces, I must recommend we go outside for help."

No one spoke in agreement. They were silent, too panicked to move. But as men they had developed the calm exterior of those who are in control. The reason they had gotten away with it for so long was that most women wanted to believe that men could really defend them with their superior stability. Most men were in fact as stable as daisies in a windstorm, and at the first sign of danger, they stopped thinking and began mouthing platitudes about national security and winning wars.

"In America there is one man of special and awesome abilities, whom I have had the distinct pleasure of working with. He belongs to their highest secret organization, used only for the most vital situations, and I believe we can get his services again precisely because it is in America's interest also not to have a war with us."

"This man you wish to see," said KGB Field Marshal Nevsky, "would he happen to be somewhat handsome, with dark hair and dark eyes and high cheekbones, and be named Remo?"

"He would," said Anna.

"And would this Remo be the same one you were seen with on several different occasions, once during a penetration of Russia and twice in America while you were on assignment there?"

"He would."

"And did this foreigner American seduce you, Comrade Chutesov?"

"No," said Anna, "I seduced him." She did not want to get entangled in men's romantic myths, so she cleared up the questions she knew were coming. "No, I am not in love with him, and yes, the sex was wonderful, and no, I am not so desperate to copulate with this man that I would destroy the planet in a nuclear holocaust."

And then KGB Field Marshal Nevsky said with absolutely typical male stupidity, "How do we know that?" She saw a few heads nod.

She would have to lie. If there was one man among them who could accept the bald-faced realistic truth, he would be a lot.

"If I want sex, who is better than a Russian man?" she said.

It was a suitable fib so that now these male leaders, all in their sixties and seventies, could allow Anna to go on with saving them from possible nuclear annihilation.

"Do what you have to do, Comrade Anna," said Nevsky.

"Thank you," she said. She was even able to keep a straight face.

She had already contacted Remo's superior, a Mr. Harold W. Smith, who for a man was extremely rational. He had explained that this phenomenon of men lusting for war was not new to Russia and had been occurring randomly around the globe.

"I must tell you, Ms. Chutesov, Remo has had no luck so far in stopping the force behind this. The man's name is Arieson. Does that ring a bell with you?"

"No," Anna had said. "But names mean nothing."

"Sometimes," said Smith. "But I don't know how helpful Remo can be."

"It is truly sad to hear that Remo has met this man and failed. However, Remo can do things that none of our people can, and he has succeeded at something no other man has managed to do."

"What's that?"

"From everything you have told me, Remo is the one man who has not been seduced into going to war under the spell of Mr. Arieson."

"That's right," Smith said.

"With my calculating ability and Remo's extraordinary powers, I think that's the best chance to get back our Russian armies."

"You may be right. But you could be wrong."

"We have nothing else available unless the Oriental, his surrogate father, wishes to help."

'No. He doesn't. He cut a deal with Arieson."

This had interested Anna, and since Remo had been present at the bargaining, Anna decided to wait until Remo arrived. He had already taken off from the U.S. when the meeting in the woods started, and

Anna waited until just before his American aircraft landed just outside Moscow to show up to greet him. She never knew which troops were loyal to whom now.

Remo in his light and smooth way almost danced down the ramp. She saw him smile when he spotted her. The KGB was undoubtedly watching her in some way. That was their custom. But she didn't care now. With Remo here, they didn't matter.

"Hello, darling," she said.

"Hello, darling," he said, and she was in his arms for a long warm kiss before she even saw his hands move.

"Not here on the tarmac," she whispered.

"Tarmac is better than a bed," he whispered.

"Where did you hear that?"

"I just made it up."

"I like it, but we are probably being photographed by the KGB."

"Good, I'll give them lessons."

"Stop that," she said, moving his arm away from one of the many points he could use to send her body into writhing pleasure. "I want you, not just fingers playing on the keyboard of my nervous system."

"I can live with that," said Remo.

"I could live for that," said Anna.

"It's good to be back with you," said Remo. He did not tell her about Poo.

"The whole country may have turned against us. It is a nightmare. We don't know which units have been infected and which have not. To make matters worse, the defecting units have seized the Premier so that they can declare war on America. They want a declaration of war. They want to give America time to get its best army into the field. They even want a place designated to fight it."

"Let's go to a hotel," said Remo. He could sense Anna's charms, and he wanted them. Her cool sparkling smile. Her delightful blue eyes. Her body that had been his in many delightful moments, and of course that great mind.

"Did you come here to save your country and mine from a disastrous war, or did you come here to make love?"

"I came here to screw," said Remo casually.

"Yes, well, let's do that after we do business."

"You women are all business," said Remo.

The facts were similar to the Vatican, the Bath, the USS *Polk*, and the Little Big Horn incidents.

A Mr. Arieson had transformed ordinary men into warriors whose only desire was to get into a battle. As with his previous appearances, there seemed to be no purpose for the war but the war itself.

"We have got to get control of our armies back into the hands of the Communist party," said Anna as her pass got her by the guards in the airport. Her Zil limousine was waiting for her for their ride back to Moscow.

"Wait a minute. I'm not putting an army into the hands of the Communist party," said Remo, the ex-marine.

"Well, where would you put it, Remo?" asked Anna. Remo was darling, Remo was exceptional, but Remo, Anna had to admit, thought like a man.

"Maybe some democratic form of government."

"Do you wish to invent one this afternoon, darling? Or did you bring one with you from America?"

"Let the people vote for the kind of government they want."

"They have. It's communist."

"Those elections are rigged."

"No, darling, it's that there is no other party running against them. The communists are the only people they can vote for or against. That's the only structure in this country. There is the Communist party or war."

"It just makes my bones rattle to give an army to communists. Communists are the biggest trouble-makers in the world. In fact, and I don't care whether you like to hear this or not, Anna, they are the main troublemakers in the world."

"You're thinking of the countries which don't have power, darling. In Russia, we are just like any other corrupt political machine. The last revolutionary was shot by Stalin. The Politburo is the safest group to run any army. They don't want to lose what they have."

"I still don't like it," said Remo.

Anna crossed her legs and gave Remo a friendly pat on the wrist, careful not to let his divine hands get her going again.

At Anna's special apartment, one with the best perks in Moscow, roughly equal to an upper-middle-class condominium in America, Remo told Anna everything he knew about Mr. Arieson.

Why, she wanted to know, did Mr. Arieson have some form of antagonism against Sinanju?

"I don't know, but Chiun seems to know. He made a deal with Arieson."

Anna nodded for Remo to go on. She poured herself a brandy in a Waterford crystal snifter and sat down on her imported French couch a cushion away from him. The night lights of Moscow glittered through her window. She had once had a fireplace but it was so badly constructed, like most buildings in Russia, that every time she tried to use it she would set fire to the building.

And only in Russia would the concrete catch fire.

She knew her country better perhaps than any of the older men and women in high positions. But none loved it better. She loved it more than she loved this marvelous man Remo, so she forced herself on this warm evening to keep her hands off him and get on with business.

Remo did not know precisely what the feud was between Sinanju and Arieson. But it went back a long way.

"How long? Ten years? Twenty years? Seventy years? I am a communist, Remo, and I think in long periods of time," said Anna.

"Three, four thousand years, I don't know."

Anna dropped the brandy snifter. It fell to the deep pile rug. Since the rug was manufactured in Russia, the crystal cracked.

"I don't understand. How can a feud go on for thousands of years?"

"The House of Sinanju has been going on since before any modern country existed, except maybe Egypt, and I do believe we've got them by a few centuries, but I don't know. Chiun knows him or knows of him, or something. He told me from the beginning that I wouldn't be able to handle him."

"You did, but that's something else."

"I didn't destroy him, though."

"No. You didn't. But you didn't join some army either."

Remo shrugged. How could he join an army knowing what he knew, being Sinanju? He could no more join an army than he could stop Sinanju working within him. He was once a marine. He understood marines. He could never be a marine again. Anna seemed interested in this. He told her about the tributes to Sinanju and the scrolls and the indentation made by a large marble thing in the mahogany floor of the treasure house of Sinanju.

He told her of his sense of connection with the frescoes in the old tunnels under Rome to that one room of the treasure house. He told her about the trip through Rome with Chiun and the pausing at the old temples.

Anna dismissed that point.

"New gods or old gods are just a waste of time. What is this thing between Sinanju and Mr. Arieson?"

"I don't know," said Remo. "And Chiun won't tell me. He's mad about the loss of the treasure, and he says knowing who Mr. Arieson is won't do any good until we get the treasure back."

"I know a bit about your surrogate father. He is quite a manipulator and the whole thing may have nothing to do with the treasure. He just wants it back. Being the standard-bearer of the world's greatest anachronism, I am sure the trappings of the past are of great importance to him."

"If it's an anachronism, why can we do things no one else can? If it's an anachronism, why don't I go running off like some idiot for war? If we're an anachronism—"

"I'm sorry, Remo, if I offended you."

"You didn't offend me. You just sounded like some communist twit. You know, just because it wasn't invented yesterday doesn't make it invalid. It's more valid because it survived the test of time."

"You indicated yourself that you were suspicious about the treasure playing any part."

"Yeah, well. That's something else," said Remo.

"The something else," said Anna wisely, "is that I am talking about your family, and you may think the worst about Chiun, but God help anyone else who thinks the same way."

"Let's get on with business. Where are these special troops?"

"We're not sure. They seem to be all over."

"Chiun usually has an idea of where he might appear. If you can get to Smitty, I can get to Sinanju. We have a special secure line," said Remo. He did not tell Anna about overlapping the American system with the Russian one in Cuba. Remo didn't understand the electronic theory exactly, only that he had overcome his little portion of it, and was proud of it.

After all, for someone who does battle with a toaster with only fifty-fifty odds of success, getting the right plug into the right socket is an accomplishment.

"All our wires are tapped by the KGB, so keep that in mind."

"Why are you warning me?"

"Because despite your marine concept of Soviet Russia, the KGB and the army and my special security service serving the Premier are not all one monolithic block out to fry your precious little buns, dear," said Anna.

"You have a sharp tongue, lady," said Remo.

"So have you when you want to," said Anna.

Remo lifted the telephone receiver off the hook. It was an old-style phone made of plastic that still had the aroma of the factory. As he got through to Smith, he polished the phone to make it look as though it were manufactured in a modern country.

Smith got the call and made the transfer to Sinanju, explaining that the signals required a lot of electronic brushing to clean them up.

Since the line was in the baker's house, Poo's mother answered the phone.

"Let me speak to Chiun, please."

"Poo is right here," said the mother.

"I want to speak to Chiun. This is business."

"Your lawfully wedded wife waits here every moment for the sound of her husband's voice. Her eyes are filled with tears. The rest of her has been filled with nothing."

"Yeah, well, let me speak to Chiun," said Remo. He was burning. He smiled at Anna. Anna smiled back.

"I will give you Poo."

"Poo, let me speak to Chiun," said Remo.

"There's another woman in the room with you," divined Poo.

"This is a business phone and I want to speak to Chiun."

"You haven't even consummated our marriage and you're cheating already," she wailed.

Anna did not understand the Oriental language Remo was using in the latter part of his call to Sinanju. But there were some things she did understand.

When Remo finally had a respite while waiting for Chiun, she asked:

"Remo, do you have a girlfriend in Sinanju?"

"No," said Remo honestly.

"Then who was that woman you were talking to?"

"What makes you think it was a woman?"

"Remo, I know how men speak to women. Who is she?"

"Not my girlfriend. Nothing to do with romance."

"Who is she, Remo?"

"My wife," said Remo. He went back to the phone. Chiun was there.

"Arieson's in Russia. He could start World War III. Where can I find him?"

"World War III is his business. Not ours. So long as he has left us Southeast Asia, I don't care."

"It's my concern. Where is he?"

"Until you get the treasure, why bother?"

"Where is he?"

"That is no way to speak to your father."

"Little Father, please tell me where he is. I am in Russia and I don't want to hang around this place looking for him."

"Well, if he were in the modern country called Russia, that must include Siberia. There is a Tartar encampment between Vladivostok and Kubsk. I would say he would probably be there. He would probably be welcome there for all the damage those little vandals are likely to do."

"Thanks, Little Father," said Remo.

"Poo has a word for you."

"I'll speak with her," said Remo, still in Korean, "only because I owe you a favor."

"Owe me a favor, Remo? You owe me everything. You just chose to pay back this one small thing. Here she is. Here, dear, don't cry. Remo does not mean to dishonor you and his own father by his failure as a man. Speak freely, Poo."

"Remo, I miss you. Come home soon."

"Thank you," said Remo, and turning to Anna, he asked her about a Tartar encampment between Vladivostok and Kubsk.

She unfolded a map on her imported glass coffee table and drew a circle encompassing thousands of miles.

"These are what we call tribal lands. It is amazing that Chiun knows of them. From the czars to us, every Russian government has allowed these people to live alone the way they wanted in total autonomy. We don't bother them and they don't bother us.

Every year, whatever government is in power delivers massive amounts of grain and feed for their horses. Even if we are starving, we deliver them grain."

"Why?" asked Remo.

"Because we want to be left alone."

"But if they use horses, why are you afraid of them?"

"Because they, Remo, are the descendants of Genghis Khan's horde."

Remo turned up his face. Sinanju knew Genghis Khan. Another military leader. Another bloodsoaksack-a-city-destroy-a-culture-go-on-with-the-bloodfest military butcher.

"You have some revulsion for Genghis Khan?" asked Anna.

"Not that much. That was someone else's problem, and that problem was taken care of."

As they arranged a flight into the restricted tribal territories, Anna said:

"You might not know this, but Genghis Khan was never defeated in battle. The horde stretched west, overrunning all the Moslem East and driving into Europe before it simply turned back."

"Yeah," said Remo as they boarded a Russian Fox three-seat fighter plane for the great eastern expanses of Russia. "I know. He overran Baghdad against Sinanju's warnings, and we took care of him."

"Genghis Khan died of a heart attack," said Anna.

"I'll show you what I mean when we get there."

The pilot was afraid to land his plane on the frozen wastes. He knew the tribal areas of Russia and knew that no pilot ever came back alive. Once, one had bailed out and certain delicate and private portions of his anatomy were left with his uniform at the tribute station.

Remo made the pilot think otherwise by getting hold of the nerves in the pilot's neck and showing him that there were worse things than death.

The pilot made a very bumpy landing. When Anna and Remo climbed out, jumping down to the frozen tundra, he took off immediately, almost crashing because he wanted to get out so quickly. Almost immediately, hundreds of horsemen in fur hats on small ponies appeared in the distance from all directions.

Anna grabbed Remo's hand.

"I'll show you the Genghis Khan heart disease," he said.

As the horsemen got closer, they seemed to drive themselves harder, as though the first to get to the intruders would be able to claim them.

The first horseman extended his hands during the ride, reaching for Remo's head. There was a Mongol game where they would fight for the head of a victim as sport. This sport was later transferred to India, where the British learned it and named it polo.

Remo caught the horseman, lightly plucking the small deadly warrior from the saddle like a ring on a carousel.

He slipped his right hand into the man's chest and through the sternum, feeling his heart collapse, his hand around the upper rib cage, blocking external movements of the heart. The man's eyes popped wide. His mouth opened in desperation, he let out a groan, and then slumped backward, his face contorted, his lips blue.

"Heart attack," said Remo to Anna, dropping the first one. He had to handle the next two simultaneously because they had arrived that way.

On one he scratched markings into the face and crushed the spleen.

"Pox," he said.

On the other, he manipulated the blood vessels in the neck until the warrior was unconscious.

"Stroke," he said.

He caught the next, and with deft movement around the rib cage, in a manner Anna could not understand, made the joints swell suddenly.

"My rheumatoid arthritis," said Remo pleasantly. "Good, but not great. Chiun's is absolutely perfect. We can do lots of other diseases but we need time for the heavyweight loss involved."

And time was what they did not have. The invincible horde was just about to close on them from all directions and Anna could not see how Remo could get them out of this one.

11

Huak the greater warrior, son of Bar, grandson of Huak Bar, great-grandson of Kar, all of whom traced their lineage to Sar Wa, who himself carried the seven-yak-tail banner of the Great Khan, Genghis himself, had lost none of his horse skills. He had not lost one flickering finger of accuracy with the short bow.

Nor did he fail to understand the gun, which his great-great-grandfather had been the first to capture from the whites.

Huak had the first flintlock taken from a Russian nobleman, whose head was strapped in a bag with a dozen scorpion beetles. He had the Enfield taken from the British troops who tried to help one of the Russian armies during its rebellion. He had the short-nosed submachine guns taken from Russian troops who got lost on their way to the border with Korea.

But his favorite weapon was the short razor-sharp sword that could take the ears off a man before he could hear the words of challenge, lie facedown, and submit.

This sword did the chunky five-foot-two-inch Huak, warrior, brandish before him, lathering his horse to reach the two whites before there was nothing left to attack.

Because Huak had taken the time to command everyone to attack the whites, because he had called out the ancient battle cry, "Let blood honor your swords," because he had been in his own mind too much of a gentleman, there would now be nothing left.

They would already be disemboweled. The ears would be gone. Someone would undoubtedly have plucked the eyes with a dagger, and as for the sexual organs of the two, those would be the first to go. There might not even be a bone left.

That was what Huak would get for being a gentleman, and as he raced his little pony, also a descendant of the horses of the horde, the only army in the world never to lose a battle, Huak the Greater thought: No more Mr. Nice Guy.

But when he was less than a spear's throw away from where the remnants should be, he saw the white man whole, the woman whole, and at least eighteen of his brothers lying peacefully in repose, numbers nineteen and twenty rapidly following suit, and with the great horse skills undiminished since the horde left the Gobi desert to devour everything and everyone in its path, Huak pulled his steed up short, almost breaking its neck.

"Skirah," he screamed, and that meant "spirit."

Huak was not afraid of death. He believed that a man killed honorably in battle would live to fight again. Only those who fled from battle died like low animals. But the spirit that came from the winds, that could snuff his soul and put him in the sleep from which his spirit would never awake—that would torment him for eternity, leave him without a horse forever, without a sword forever, and steal his name so Huak would not even know who he was but be like some grain of sand, nothing, undifferent from any other, unbeing.

A few were not in time to hear his warning about the evil wind spirit, and went to sleep at the spirit's hands. He had brought his pale woman with him, probably also to feast on the souls of those to be made like dust, like sand, like nothing.

Of those gone before the other horses were able to rein in, the number was twenty-two, not dead so much as lost forever.

A young warrior, hearing Huak's command, but thinking there were so many of them that the white man could not possibly dodge a hundred arrows, pulled back his bow in the quick short draw of the bowstring made famous at the gates of Baghdad and at the fringes of Europe.

Huak's knife cut that short with a snap jab into the jugular. The boy fell instantly like an old wineskin spilling its red contents on the tundra.

The boy's father, riding adjacent to the son, saw what Huak had done, and said:

"Thank you, brother Huak." And no more was said. The father understood that if the son had died at the spirit's hands, his soul would be gone forever. Now they could take the body back with them and bury it knowing it was still part of them, possibly returning even in the next birth, a boy of course.

Male spirits never came back as women. Thus was the belief of the horde unchanged in its centuries of unbroken triumph.

A thousand horses came to snorting, stamping rest around the two whites. Clouds of warm air from their nostrils puffed out into the cold Siberian air.

"Oh Skirah spirit, what have you come for, what

can we give you to appease you, to honor you so that
you will leave our souls in peace and seek others?"

"Get your horses back, they smell. The whole horde
smells like a shit farm," said the white man in the
older tongue used at the time of Genghis Khan
himself.

"How many languages do you speak?" whispered
Anna. She had seen Remo kill before, and all of it
looked so smooth, it could have been someone stacking crates at an hourly wage.

"I dunno," answered Remo in English. "You read
the scrolls, you pick up dozens of languages. Sinanju
needed them for work."

"I presume, darling, that's Mongolian," said Anna.

"No. The horde spoke a dialect peculiar to Genghis Khan's tribe."

"How many words do you know?"

"If you know to tell them to move their smelly
horses back, you've got fifty percent of everything
you ever need to tell a Mongol," said Remo, and in
the language Chiun had taught him during a training session outside Dayton, Ohio, while Remo was
still learning basic breath, he said:

"Horses, move backward. Back. And you there.
Clean up the droppings. Don't litter the tundra. Bunch
of dirty dogs. Back."

A warrior dismounted, and quickly gathered a loose
plop of goo in a skin.

"You didn't have to use your hands. We may be
eating supper with you. On second thought, if you've
only got yak meat, we'll do without. I'm looking for
someone."

"Whom, Skirah, do you seek?"

"He calls himself Mr. Arieson and I think he should
be around here."

"Arieson?"

"Thick neck. Beard. Blazing eyes. Hard to put a spear through. Probably impossible."

"Oh, you mean our friend Kakak."

"White?" asked Remo.

"What else is the color of ugly dead flesh?" asked Huak.

"Do you want to stay on that horse or would you like to blend in with the tundra?" said Remo.

"I did not mean to dishonor your color, Skirah. Come with us and take your glorious bride spirit with you. Our encampment is not far away."

"Ride ahead and clear the horses out. I don't want to be downwind from you guys."

"As you say, Skirah," said Huak to Remo.

"Who is Skirah?" asked Anna.

"One of their spirits. Maybe the way they pronounce Sinanju."

"I think I understand. Religion, spirits, and gods are the way people explain to themselves what they don't understand. So when Genghis Khan died at the hands of Sinanju, they explained it away as a bad spirit. And it had to be a great bad spirit because Genghis Khan was great. It's all logical. Everything in the world is logical, except we don't always understand the logic right away. Don't you think?"

"We're walking behind eight hundred horses, and you're thinking about rational explanations for myths?" asked Remo.

"What should I be thinking about?"

"Where you're stepping," said Remo.

Anna felt a sudden warm moistness up around the calf of her boot. She realized Remo could be brilliant at times.

But there was something far more sinister on the tundra. As they approached the encampment, great gaping cracks appeared around them, parallel paths

chewing up the frost-white earth, churning up frozen blackness underneath. Something had passed
here very recently, and it used treads. Tanks.

But the Mongols of the horde did not use tanks, at
least not to Anna's knowledge. With modern equipment like that, these horsemen—invincible in the
frozen wastes of Siberia—could theoretically overrun
Europe, something they could not do with Genghis
Khan.

Then again, the family that had stopped him was
back again. He might stop them before they broke
out.

Unless, thought Anna, the treads were not made
by Mongol-driven tanks at all. Maybe it is something
worse.

And as soon as they saw the encampment, Anna
knew the worst had happened. Walking freely among
the Mongols were Russian soldiers and officers. Thousands of them. She saw them with their arms around
the shoulders of the Mongols, and vice versa.

That meant the prohibition against whites was not
universal. The Russian soldiers had somehow earned
the friendship of the Mongols, and considering the
Mongol mentality and the military mentality, she was
fairly certain how it happened.

"Remo, ask the leader why they are friendly with
Russians now."

She heard Remo call out to the backs of the hundreds of horsemen and one of them turned around
and galloped back. She heard Remo ask questions in
that strange tongue and saw many hand motions on
the part of the Mongol.

Remo translated as the Mongol spoke.

"There was a great battle, not in numbers but in
spirit. The whites showed they did not fear death.

They only feared dishonor. They showed a love of battle and a love of war."

Anna nodded. It was all coming together now.

Remo continued:

"They did not fight as whites ordinarily do, to steal something, to protect something, or just to save their miserable lives. They fought for the honor of fighting. These are the first whites who understood war."

"He mentioned that name for Arieson. Kakak."

"No," said Remo. "That is their name for war. Mr. Arieson, I guess quite logically, means war."

"That's the only thing he seems to mean," said Anna. So elements of the Russian army had joined the Mongol horde. And she was fairly certain how they would pull off this war with America. And they just might win it, even without the use of nuclear weapons.

They could pour over the Bering Strait supported by ships from the Vladivostok naval station that had sailed north. It would not be easy, but since America always suspected an attack against Europe and not its own borders, then they could be taken by surprise. What forces did America have to oppose the Russians? Nothing but what was in Alaska, and the trek up through Canada would be almost as long as Russia's trek to its borders. They could battle down through Canada, and with the spirit of these soldiers, they could just as well win.

What was she thinking? Was she insane? Was she so marrow-deep a Russian that she thought they would win something by conquering America?

How could they occupy a country of two hundred and forty million, moving their forces not only through Siberian transit but down across Canada as well? They would also have to conquer Canada. And should that even be possible, should moving the troops be as easy as moving from Minsk to Pinsk, why on earth would they think that occupying America would do them any good? To be free of a competitor with nuclear weapons? There would surely be another, and if Russia should attain its age-old dream of conquering the world, anyone who knew how men traditionally ran things had to understand that the world would have to split up into two camps and there could just as easily be a war between Russia East and Russia West.

No, this had to be stopped here. This had to be stopped now. And she was grateful that the man beside her, this glorious, handsome, wonderful anachronism, was the only man to do it.

As for Mr. Arieson, she was sure there was a logical explanation for this creature that had not occurred to Remo or his rather intelligent superior, Harold W. Smith.

Remo understood the world of the extent of the human body. Smith understood things mostly in the great world of technology, but no one yet had brought common rational sense to Mr. Arieson.

It was she who had been able to understand that for some reason, Remo and his surrogate father, Chiun, were immune to Arieson's blandishments. It was she who understood that the only reason Remo felt he had failed was that he had not enjoyed the total victory Sinanju was used to.

And it was going to be Anna Chutesov who would figure out what Mr. Arieson's real weaknesses were.

She had never failed with any other man. There was no reason to start failing now.

And yet, Anna was not prepared for what she saw.

Riding on a little pony was a man so apparently
powerful that power became a handsomeness the
like of which she had never seen. His presence almost took her breath away. His beard seemed a
perfect accessory for his strong jaw and muscled
neck. His eyes had a glow of infinity to them. And
he wore a simple Russian soldier's helmet, making it
more glorious by his presence underneath it than
any helmet on any soldier she had ever seen. She
understood now why men could feel a glorious call
to battle in his presence, and she hadn't even spoken
to him yet.

"Here comes the spoilsport, men. Here he comes,
sauntering after the fine cavalry. Come on, ruin it all
for everyone."

This from Mr. Arieson, the voice carrying over a
thousand tents and filling the slight valley in this
wasteland.

"Look, already the horses are clearing out just
because he doesn't want them. Glad to see you're
here, Remo. You're not going to get me, but here
you come nevertheless, empty-handed, despite the
deal your father made."

"I see you don't mind the smell of horses," Remo
called out. The entire camp stopped to look at the
two men facing each other, taunting each other.

"Have you ever smelled a battlefield two days after? The rotting bodies would make you pass out."

"So why are you trying to start a war?" Remo
called out. He made sure Anna was to the side as he
walked steadily toward Arieson.

"Who said I didn't like the smell? I love it. I said
you'd pass out. I'd roll around in it and make sure
people built statues there so they wouldn't remember how horrible it was, and think they really accomplished something."

A tank commander, hearing Mr. Arieson yell insults at the lone stranger, thought he would do a favor for this man who had given him the gift of heroism by running over the skinny white man who seemed not to need heavy winter clothes. He turned his massive ground-chewing machine toward the man and drove. He heard Mr. Arieson call out that it wouldn't do any good, that it never had, but the man now filled with the true spirit of battle was ready to die trying.

He charged his behemoth down on the thin figure and the man didn't bother to dodge, but like a bull-fighter stepped to the side, cleaved off a tread barehanded, then cleaved off the other tread as the tank spun helplessly around.

The tank commander, enraged at losing his armor-plated chariot, stormed out with his sidearm and a knife, and promptly found out what they tasted like as the thin stranger stuffed them down his throat and kept walking.

"See, it won't do anyone any good," called out Arieson. "That is an assassin. No soldier there. A Sinanju assassin. No glory there. Death in the night. Highest bidder gets the service. No courage in that man. Doesn't even fight fear. Uses it. No courage there, assassin."

"Is that true, Remo? Is that what is different?" said Anna.

"I have fear. I just use it. He's right."

"Look, let's talk to Mr. Arieson."

"I don't want to talk. I want to nail him."

"Have you tried talking?"

"You can't talk with a man who loves the smell of rotting bodies."

"But you haven't, have you?"

"I'll kill him, then I'll talk to him," said Remo, thinking that since his body blows had proved ineffective he might try hurling a soldier or two at Arieson's head and see what that produced.

"Very bright, Remo. Are you good at talking to the dead?"

"I mean when he's dead he won't be a problem anymore."

"You haven't succeeded yet. Just let me talk to him."

"Don't make it too long," said Remo.

"Why don't you fight some people while you're waiting?" said Anna.

"Are you being sarcastic?"

"Partly, but I want to understand his reactions to you. They're very interesting."

Close to Arieson, Anna sensed an inner laughter at everything that went on, almost as though he cared but didn't care. Several soldiers issued a challenge to Remo. Arieson called out that it wouldn't do any good, that the soldiers would die against Sinanju, that by the evening their commanders would be dead, and they would no longer be an army.

Sinanju had done this countless times throughout history.

"Were you there?" asked Anna.

"If you want to undress and dance for my glory, fine. But ask me questions?"

"Why not?" asked Anna.

"You just did it again."

"You made a deal with Remo's surrogate father. Perhaps I can help you make a deal with Remo."

"How do you deal with someone who is Sinanju and doesn't respect what he's dealing with?"

Remo cleaved Russian commandos with a backhand so slow it looked as though the hand itself was drawn out of his body. The soldiers went in separate directions, heads going one way, legs another. Anna turned away from the slaughter.

"No fair fight from Sinanju," called out Arieson. "Bunch of assassins."

"So Remo has some form of power over you," said Anna.

"Not over me. Over what I want to do. He gets in the way. These Sinanju boys have been doing that for centuries."

"And you've been around for centuries," said Anna. Arieson's strong legs seemed to caress the fat belly of the little horse. She wondered if the horse enjoyed it. She wondered if she would enjoy it. What was it about this man that so stimulated sexual desire in her? Remo did the same thing to her, but for a good reason. She had known the wonders he could deliver. All she knew about Arieson was that he could transform ordinary soldiers into valiant warriors.

The Mongols were avoiding the fight with Remo. Only the Russians kept coming on at him. She did not like to see this kind of killing. For the soldiers it was some form of glory. But she knew Remo might not even be thinking about what was going on except to be concentrating on the form of the blow to keep in good practice.

"What do you want, Mr. Arieson?"

"What does Remo want?" asked Arieson.

"The treasure of Sinanju," said Anna. The words were out almost immediately, but she knew she was right. Everything else had been a stalemate.

"Oh, that. The greedy rewards for murder."

"You made a deal with Chiun. Maybe I can broker a deal with Remo. I know he wants the treasure."

Anna heard something roll nearby. She hoped it wasn't a head.

She turned to Remo.

"Will you stop that, Remo?" she yelled.

"I didn't start anything. They're coming at me," Remo called back.

"Well, just stop it," she said, and turned away so she wouldn't see what would happen to three burly tankers who had now grabbed large steel wrenches and were going to try to beat the slim stranger with the thick wrists.

"I didn't start it," said Remo. "They were coming at me."

He was by her side now, looking up at Arieson.

"Do you want the treasure of Sinanju?" asked Arieson.

"I do."

"What will you give me for it? Will you make the same deal as Chiun?"

"No," said Remo. "But I'm going to get the Premier and end this horde forever. We should have done it at the fringes of Europe when we took care of your boy Genghis Khan. Should have done the job right."

"Leave my horde alone. I've felt at home here more than with any other army."

"I don't want my country to be in a war with Russia."

"All right. All right. I'll go. There won't be a war. Will that make you happy?"

"Yeah."

"Okay, if that's your horrible price. You can have it this time. But I warn you, you can't stop me forever, especially now that I know you want the treasure of Sinanju."

"Do you know where it is?" asked Remo.

"Of course I do."

"How?" asked Remo.

"Ah," said Arieson, and it sounded like all the winds over all the deserts and all the battlefields that had ever been. And he sat no more on the Mongol pony before them. The pony whinnied and then scampered away, only to be brought quickly to rein by a young Mongol horseman in this forbidden encampment in the Siberian wasteland.

There was a silence all around them. Something important was no longer there, and neither Remo nor Anna knew what it was. Something seemed to go out of the Russian soldiers. There was no more bounce or joy or comradeship with the Mongols. They seemed like a bunch of men in uniforms stuck in a cold inhospitable place they would like to escape.

Only the Mongols seemed to stay the same, as a priest called out that Mr. Arieson remained in their hearts always.

"Anna, Anna," came the voice from a yak tent. A handsome bald-headed man wearing an ill-fitting Russian soldier's uniform was waving to Anna and Remo.

Remo recognized the face from the newspapers. It was the Russian Premier. "Anna, what are you doing here?"

"What are you doing here?" she answered.

"We are about to launch the greatest campaign in Russian history. Read this," he said. It was a piece of parchment with the Communist-party insignia on it.

Anna knew what it was. These things had not been seen for centuries, not since the advent of the sneak attack.

It was a declaration of war against America and it bore the Premier's signature. Arieson had gotten to the head of the Communist party as well as the soldiers. Here was a man who should have known better. He had lost his entire family in the great patriotic war in which Russia had defeated the lunacy of Nazi Germany.

Anna tore it up.

"What are you doing?"

"It's all over."

"It can't be. I was going to conquer America," said the Premier.

"Excuse me," said Remo. He stepped in between Anna and the Premier, and with limited power and maximum palm exposure slapped the Premier hard, like a giant towel whacking water. The Premier's eyes teared momentarily, then a silly smile appeared on his face. He sniffled back the sudden nosebleed.

"Friendship always between the glorious freedom-loving American people and their allies, the glorious Russian people enjoying the fruits and luxuries of socialism," said the Premier.

The Russian soldiers, getting back to normal, now began to fear the Mongols again, and the Mongols, sensing it, began closing in. But Remo called out that his protection was upon them, and so he, Anna, and the Premier, with the defecting army units, made their way that day out of the special tribal encampments reserved for the notorious horde of Genghis Khan.

Harold W. Smith received word from his Russian contact, Anna Chutesov, that the danger of imminent war was now over. But according to the pattern of this new force, it would reappear again. This he had to stress.

"Yes, but we're learning more about him, Mr. Smith. We are learning Remo has something he wants."

"And what's that?"

"Remo and Sinanju have been in his way for centuries."

"But he, whatever he is, whoever he is, is still around."

"Ah, but Mr. Smith, you are missing the most salient point. So is Sinanju."

In Anna's apartment they made love on a fur rug, with the apartment dark, with the quiet lights of Moscow beaming in the near distance, their bodies becoming one, until Anna with delirious joy shrieked the completion of her ecstasy.

"You're wonderful, Remo."

"Fair. My mind's elsewhere," said Remo.

"You didn't have to tell me that."

"I don't mean to insult you, but lovemaking is part of my skills. Sometimes they're good and sometimes they're fair, just like other strokes. It doesn't mean I don't care."

"Was it work for you, Remo?"

"With you it's never work, Anna."

"I hope so," she said. "But you know, I'll never know."

"You know," he said, kissing her gently. But she was right. Sometimes he didn't know either. When you were Sinanju, when you became a Master, Sinanju was not something you used or did not use; it was what you were.

When he had seen Mr. Arieson, there was no choice about whether he would be enthralled or not. He was disgusted, just as he would be disgusted by a bad smell. It was not a choice. His antagonism toward that force was as central to him as his breathing. And Remo did not know why.

The little half-tinkle of the second-rate Russian

phone rang above them on a table. Remo reached
back to get it without disturbing anything.

"That was well done," laughed Anna.

It was Chiun, who had been told that Mr. Arieson
was about to give back the treasure of Sinanju to
Remo, if Remo would meet him at a special place, a
place dear to his heart.

"All right. I'll make it there in a while."

"What could be more important than the treasure of
Sinanju?"

"Litte Father, I'll get the treasure, but in a short
while."

"I know what you're doing and your white lust for
a white body has overcome the good judgment and
training I have spent the best years of my life giving
you."

"I am talking about less than a few minutes," said
Remo.

"You are talking about uncontrollable, dirty lust
for that white Russian hussy, instead of faithfulness
to your precious wife, Poo."

"I'll get the treasure, Little Father," said Remo,
hanging up.

The place Arieson had picked was a complex of
miles and miles of underground concrete bunkers
fronted by miles and miles of rotting concrete tank
traps. It stretched along the border of France and
Germany, a massive undertaking equal in its time to
the pyramids.

It was, however, perhaps the greatest failure of all
time.

It was the Maginot Line, too expensive now for
France to even dismantle, but in its time it had loomed
as the greatest defensive network ever assembled. It
stared Germany in the face. France made foreign
policy confidently behind its fortifications. When Ger-

many attacked Poland, France stood by its poor ally. It also stood behind its Maginot Line.

Germany went around it.

No one in France had thought of that.

France fell.

The Second World War was on, the Maginot Line was dead forever.

Inside its coffinlike interior, Mr. Arieson now waited, whistling joyfully. He glowed in the dark. He tossed in his hands a large vase emblazoned with pink flamingos. Each flamingo held a gold rod with a diamond on top, the archaic but distinct sign of a minor dynasty Remo recognized.

He had seen it sitting on velvet amid thirty or so other vases, all quite similar. He had never seen it anywhere else but in that one place, because that minor dynasty had been absorbed entirely by the country that would become China.

The place he had seen this vase before was in the treasure house of Sinanju. Arieson handed Remo the vase.

"You can have the rest, too. Just give me Chiun's deal," said Arieson.

Remo could see his outlines in the dark even if a faint glow did not emanate from him. Anna, however, had difficulty walking in the dark because she needed strong light to see. Remo held the precious vase in one hand and steadied Anna with the other.

Arieson waited, chuckling and whistling. Something was shaking the concrete underground bunker. It felt like there was traffic overhead. Lots of traffic. One truck after another, rolling along over their heads.

"Your choice, Remo. Just clear out and I'll tell you where the treasure was hidden a few years ago. Bring it back to Chiun, both of you enjoy the fruits of thousands of years of troublemaking, emperor-killing, conqueror-stopping, whatever you wish. Yours. Feel it."

Remo could feel the old glaze in his hand. Chiun appreciated this period perhaps more than any other. Did Arieson know that? There was some dirt at the base. There had never been dirt at the base.

The truck sounds were getting heavier.

Arieson was getting happier.

"What's going on up there?"

"If you take the treasure, it won't matter. Feels good, doesn't it, son?"

"You mean I have to clear out of Europe?"

"Now especially."

"What's going on up there?"

"A golden oldie," sighed Arieson. "One of my favorites."

"A war?"

"Not a dance," sang Mr. Arieson. "Think about it. Here you will be returning to Sinanju as the Master who recovered the treasure. You'll be somebody. Think of Chiun. Think of his gratitude. Think of you having the upper hand."

Remo was thinking about getting out of the marriage to Poo, among other things. He was too experienced to know that returning the treasure would end Chiun's complaining. Chiun was only happy when complaining. The words "All right, a deal" were almost out of his mouth when he said:

"I think I'd better see what's going on upstairs."

"Don't bother to look. A group of valiant French officers has decided to regain the honor of France humiliated so many times by the dastardly Hun. The dastardly Hun is going to be up there also. You don't know how hard it's been for me. We're going on almost fifty years now without a Franco-German war. A generation without a Franco-German war is like a night without stars."

"Remo," said Anna, "you can't let another one of these disasters happen. You can't let millions die just for your treasure. Remo?"

"Hold on," said Remo, whose marriage to Poo was still valid in Sinanju if nowhere else on earth. "I'm thinking."

12

It was not an easy choice, and the shortage of time didn't make it easier. On one hand were the assured deaths of thousands of civilized Europeans, who after years of regularly killing each other in warfare had finally learned to live together. On that side was death, the destruction of major cities, perhaps even this time an end to one of the nations, each of which when they were not warring had produced so much for the benefit of mankind and would continue to do so.

On the other was the treasure of Sinanju. Actually, when Remo thought about it, there really wasn't much choice. There were always going to be wars. If not the French and Germans, then certainly the Arabs and Iranians, the Arabs and the Israelis, the Arabs and the Africans, the Arabs and the Arabs. And that was just one ethnic group. Moving on from the Semites, you couldn't get out of the Asian subcontinent without another good twenty wars.

So what was he stopping, really?

"Remo, why are you taking so long?" asked Anna. "Are you going to let the French and Germans slaughter each other again?"

"Eh," said Remo.

"Is that your answer to warfare? A blasé little 'eh'? That's it?"

Remo shrugged.

"Trust me, Remo. I think I have figured out what Mr. Arieson must be. I don't think he's invincible. Don't make the deal with him. I'll help you with the treasure. You've never had the combined might of both Russia and America working for you. I think Mr. Arieson has made a mistake by returning part of the treasure. Remo, stop this war."

Arieson, who had let Anna have her full say, finally interrupted. His voice resonated throughout the bunker like a hymn, like trumpets, like all the music men had ever used to raise their hearts to the battle. Anna was not unaware of this. She sensed Remo was. Moisture had collected on the concrete walls in the old Maginot Line and it was like breathing in a sewer. In a war, men would fight in bunkers like these and worse. All the martial music could not change that. She squeezed Remo's arm as Arieson spoke.

"Remo, have you ever really seen an old-fashioned war? I mean a good one. Not something where the cities are bombed, and drably dressed men crawl through the mud, and no one even knows where the enemy is half the time. I'm not talking about that shoddy new stuff. I'm talking good old-fashioned war, with banners and trumpets and men in glorious uniforms marching out to make history and glory."

"And to hack away at each other like butchers and then have their poets cover it up," said Remo. "I've read about those kinds."

"Once a Sinanju assassin, always a Sinanju assassin. What about the deal? You don't care about these armies. You've always considered warriors as some kind of cheap competition for your services."

"You don't mean to tell us you've been around for thousands of years," said Anna.

"I'm not talking to you, girlie," said Arieson. "What about it, Sinanju boy? Take the deal. You get the treasure. All you people ever cared about was getting paid. Don't feel you have to show off for the girl."

"Remo!" cried Anna.

"I was still raised by the nuns. I was still raised American," said Remo. "No deal."

It was not an attack so much as an eerie light and voices from nowhere that lunged toward Remo. But Remo held the vase. He held the vase against the strange sense of flesh that was not flesh, energy that was more thought than energy, against hands that were not hands trying to take back the vase that had once been given in tribute to the Masters of Sinanju.

And then Arieson was gone and Remo had a war to stop.

It was not hard. Everything seemed to fall apart when Arieson left anyhow, and this time when Arieson was gone both France and Germany closed in on what they called their lunatic commanders, who instead of being considered saviors of the nations were both publicly called "lunatic disasters who never should have been given command of troops."

But Remo was left with one vase in the sunlight of a French field where ugly concrete lay too vast to be removed.

"I don't think Chiun's going to let me out of the marriage to Poo for one stinking vase, Anna," said Remo. "And I don't blame him. I had the treasure in my hands for a single deal for one more lousy war that these yo-yos probably would have loved to fight anyhow, and I let it go. I may have let Chiun down. I may have let down every Master in the line."

"Let me see the vase," said Anna.

Remo started to brush off the dirt before he handed it to her, but Anna, horrified, told him to leave the dirt.

"That's our chance. That's what I'm counting on. Arieson left the earth. I'm surprised he did so."

"Dirt is something you clean off," said Remo. "Chiun won't be happy he's getting only one vase back, let alone a dirty one."

"Dirt is what things are buried in. Dirt is what is peculiar to each place, dirt is what the greatest technological nation on the earth can read a speck of and tell you exactly where it came from."

"We have to go back to Russia?"

"Are you kidding? I'm talking about modern science. Your Harold Smith has at his disposal the greatest technological materials known to man. He's your best chance."

None of them talked directly to the scientist in the mass-spectrometry laboratory because that would have given him an inkling of whom he might be working for. Instead, through concealed cameras they watched as another scientist who thought he was working on a government grant for archaeological expeditions talked to the operator of the instrument. They could have gotten a report, but they didn't even want to wait that long.

Anna was amazed how all this could be accomplished in such secret openness. They did the watching in the back of a limousine, which had microscopic controls that gave this one brilliant man access to more technological power than perhaps any human being other than his president.

Anna appreciated how America had chosen well in Harold W. Smith, the taciturn lemon-faced head of

Remo's organization. Harold W. Smith was not one to believe in the Red Menace. He understood her country as an enemy. He understood he had to use caution and stamp out its thrusts toward his own country, but he did not view Russia as the demon of the world. He was not one to start a war, but this man was sure to finish it.

Remo was bored with the spectrometry research and kept reaching a hand to her knee. Anna liked the hand on her knee but she did not want an orgasm while discussing earth samples with someone else in the back seat of an American limousine.

They were driving down the Merritt Parkway just outside New York City. The driver was sealed off by a solid soundproof glass shield. They could hear him but he could not hear them unless they gave him an order through a microphone. To the world it looked like a common luxury automobile where the inhabitants were watching television.

The impressive reading of particles in the laboratory was not done through some lens, but rather by bombarding the earth with electrons and reading the emissions on a printout.

They heard the technologist read the structure of the earth found on the vase.

The archaeologist-geographer punched the readings into a portable computer he carried. Both men were dressed as though they were about to go out and throw a Frisbee for a while. They looked so ordinary doing such an extraordinary thing, thought Anna.

She slapped Remo's wonderfully skilled hand again. "Please," she said. Harold W. Smith blushed.

"Nothing," said Remo. "I wasn't doing anything. If I did something, you would feel this—"

"Remo!" shrieked Anna.

"Remo, please," said Smith, trying to avert his eyes.

"Nothing," said Remo, raising his hands as an innocent.

And then the findings.

The computer announced three places the earth could have come from, but Remo knew immediately that two were wrong. One was along the coast of Chile, and the other was a fishing village in Africa.

"I always wondered how they managed to move so much treasure and only find witnesses who saw it leave the village, while no one anywhere saw it arrive. I always wondered how Chiun could have sifted through North Korean intelligence without finding the men who had lugged it away. I always wondered," said Remo.

Anna and Smith said the third place was not only a brilliant site but also logical.

It was as brilliant as it was simple. Smith and Anna discussed Arieson as they all three drove to a small military airport outside of New York City. They had the treasure. Now to end the power of Mr. Arieson.

Cymbals of welcome reached Remo and Anna as they arrived at the junction of Sinanju One with Sinanju Two and Three, an area which looked like a large empty parking lot. It stopped at a mud path, Sinanju proper.

Chiun was waiting, too, squinting disapproval.

"You have brought her here. Into your own village. A white. That white. The white you have consorted with," said Chiun, looking at Anna.

"You'll never guess where the treasure is."

"Of course I'll never guess. If I could have guessed, I would have found it."

"Do you think that is a nice hillock you are standing on, Little Father?" asked Remo.

"It overlooks the highway. Behind me, down the path into the village, I can see everything going on there. It is a perfect spot."

"And on the night the treasure was stolen, did not the North Korean intelligence operatives carry the treasure up this path?"

"It is the only way to get out of Sinanju. Why not? Don't try to escape the fact that you have brought that," said Chiun, pointing at Anna, "back to where you live, where your precious wife lives."

"I know about that marriage. It's not a real one," said Anna with a cold smile.

"And Remo said you were intelligent," laughed Chiun. "They tell that to all you girls."

"I believe Remo wouldn't lie."

"Believe what you want," said Chiun, "but you'll never know."

"Getting back to the treasure, Little Father, did it not seem strange to you that you could uncover none of the many men who hauled it away?" asked Remo.

"If they could have been found, I would have found them. As a precaution, obviously they were killed so they would not tell."

'Ah, and when were they killed? Where were they killed?"

"I don't like these games."

"You played games with Mr. Arieson. You didn't tell me."

"I'm allowed. I'm your father," said Chiun.

"Isn't it amazing how that hill you are on seems to grow?" Anna said.

"Of course it grows. It is the Sinanju garbage dump."

"And at the bottom, where the dump touches the once-fresh earth, you will find the poisoned bodies of the men who hauled away your treasure."

"Good. Let them rot," said Chiun.

"Sir, if they are dead, who carried the treasure farther, and why do I think they were poisoned?"

"Because you are a sex-crazed white woman and never had a logical thought in your head," said Chiun.

"They were poisoned, I am sure, because that was the quietest way to get rid of them after they did their work, and then one man with a shovel could cover them with the loose garbage and drive back to Pyongyang, where he could agree to come to your village as often as you want to help you look for the treasure. Your treasure has been in the only one safe place it could have been hidden all along. Right here in Sinanju."

Anna thought Chiun was so excited about the find that he did not remember to thank her, but Remo explained Chiun had difficulty with thanks. This of course did not mean that anyone could ever forget to thank Chiun. When it came to gratitude, he was very careful to weigh and measure.

The entire village dug into the little garbage heap, some with shovels, some with their bare hands. They sang as they worked, about the glory of their House of Sinanju.

But they always sang as they worked while the Masters of Sinanju were around. Chiun did not forget nor let them forget that when he was gone earning tribute for the entire village, they had not lifted a finger when the treasure was stolen.

They covered their faces when they came down to the decomposing bodies, but under the bodies was fresh, easily dug earth, and only the thinnest layer of earth covered the first trunk of valuables. All night

they cleaned and carried and hauled, while Chiun
directed one group here and one there to lay the
treasures before the doorway of the House of Sinanju.
He and Remo would put them where they belonged.
This for Remo and Chiun would be a labor of love.

"May I come in?" asked Anna. She had helped
locate the treasure. She had saved it for Remo and
Chiun. She was actually feeling good for the cranky
old racist.

"No," said Chiun.

"I do believe I was instrumental in your regaining
the historical treasure that meant so much to your
lines of assassins," said Anna.

"You had some deal with Remo. Probably for sex,"
said Chiun.

"No. I stopped a war," said Remo, making sure
the Mayan gold was not mixed with the lighter and
shinier Thai gold.

Chiun was proud that Remo would remember the
difference between the two.

"Well, we can deal with Arieson now."

"I've heard about your deals, Chiun. What are you
going to give him now?" asked Anna.

"A pinch of something or other," said Chiun. He
had spotted the casks of faience beads from the
Third Dynasty of the upper kingdom of the Nile.
"To the left, along with the alabaster cats, thank
you," he said to the Sinanju workers.

"You don't understand, Master of Sinanju, Arieson
is not some mindless mystical thing that you could
understand. Smith, an extremely intelligent and per-
ceptive man, and I have put our heads together."

"Twin cabbages," said Chiun, seeing the great dam-
ask cloth, named for the city of its origin, Damascus.
"Ah, the beautiful Abbasids," said Chiun, being reminded of the treachery of that dynasty. And then of

course there were the treasures from Baghdad, the pinnacle of civilization, which the warrior Genghis Khan destroyed, and then of course died for that abomination.

"The old Baghdad," said Chiun, taking a bolt of silk centuries old but still perfect because of the denseness of its weave and the special perfection of its silkworms fed a secret diet by the wonderful caliphs in that wonderful city.

And of course, the gifts from the Greek tyrants, coming now over the hill, down the path toward the House of Sinanju. Chiun's hands were aflutter with joy. The Masters of Sinanju always had special affection for the Greek tyrants. While the Greeks never paid excessively, they always understood exactly the work they wanted. They were not ones to see imaginary plots behind every marble wall. They knew who had to be removed and got the best to do it, saving themselves much wealth in the long run.

"Mr. Arieson," said Anna, "in case you are interested, is an electronic force that feeds off its victims themselves. The victims are human beings who respond to negative military impulses. The reason you and Remo cannot be affected is you are so perfectly trained that all your basic responses are harnessed. Other men fight their fear; your fear powers you. You fight nothing because you are one with every element of yourselves. Do you understand?"

"You slept with a woman who is going to explain Sinanju to you?" asked Chiun.

Remo made a motion of the inexplicability of women, and stopped the Mali iron statues before they were brought too far forward.

"Those go back a bit," said Remo.

"Are you coming?" asked Anna.

"No, he's not," said Chiun.

"Let him answer," said Anna.

"I've got to put stuff away here first."

"Don't you want to see Mr. Arieson collapse in an electronic counterforce?"

"Sure, but I've got to straighten up the rooms first," said Remo. Chiun smiled. Remo could be a good boy at times. And Remo was his.

"He knows your little tricks cannot stop someone like Arieson," Chiun said.

"But he's not a someone. That's what Smith and I figured out, from all the evidence."

Chiun laughed. "You will never stop him. I will make you a bargain. If you in your ways stop Arieson, you may have Remo. If not, never set foot here again."

"You won't interfere with us because I'm white?" asked Anna.

"I promise," said Chiun.

"Hey, you can't promise me to anyone," said Remo.

"I can promise not to interfere," said Chiun.

"Done," said Anna.

"Done," said Chiun.

"I'll phone for you, Remo."

"Say good-bye to her, Remo."

But Remo ignored them both. Anna did not see it as she walked up the mud path toward the now lower hill at the entrance, but Remo did and he knew where it went. He had seen pictures like it in the tunnels under Rome. He watched three men laboriously carry it on their shoulders, but he ran out to help them. Holding the marble base lightly in his fingers, he alone walked the path back to the house, and wiping his feet free of mud he carried it into the house and into the room where its square marble base fit exactly into the indentation in the dark mahogany.

It was a marble bust. And the face had a beard and a fat neck, and obviously, four hundred years before the birth of Christ, Mr. Arieson had posed for it.

It took three days for Remo and Chiun to replace the treasure. During that time, word reached Poo that Remo, in payment for returning the treasure of Sinanju, was released from his marriage vows.

She came up to the house. She wept at the doorway. She wept louder when other villagers were about. She tore her hair. She screamed insults and curses. She said there would not be a soul in Sinanju who would not know how Remo had failed in his manhood in regard to her.

This was not much of a threat because everyone knew that on the wedding night anyhow. Poo had always been a bigmouth.

Poo stretched her great bulk over the steps of the doorway to the House of Sinanju, known in Sinanju as the House of the Masters, and declared to one and all she was an abandoned woman.

"When does this stop, Little Father?" asked Remo.

"On the fifth day," said Chiun.

"Why the fifth day?" asked Remo.

"By the fifth day she will be tired and ready," said Chiun, without explaining ready for what.

On the fifth day, Chiun went down to where Poo lay exhausted and whispered in her ear. She allowed him to help her up and walk her back down to her home in the village.

"Done," said Chiun on his return to the house.

"What did you say to her?" asked Remo.

"Forty-two thousand dollars cash," said Chiun. "What did you think I said to her? That everything would be all right? That the marriage was over? That she was better off without you?"

"That's a lot of money," said Remo.

"She earned it," said Chiun. "It was truly a noble performance she did on our steps."

"How sure are you we won't hear from Anna Chutesov?" asked Remo.

"Did the statue fit the room exactly, and was not the likeness perfect?"

"Yes," said Remo.

"Be confident, she will never come here again," said Chiun.

"That's not what I wanted, Little Father."

"You wanted to eat red meat at one time also," said Chiun.

"But Anna's different. She's special."

"You only feel she's special."

"That's the only feel I care about, Chiun," said Remo.

"Right," said Chiun. "You don't care what I think. You don't care what is good for the House of Sinanju, but what does the great Remo Williams feel? The feelings that count here are mine," said Chiun. And walking through the rooms of the house, he kept repeating the word "mine," although each time he said it the word became softer, and happier, as he viewed the returned treasure of Sinanju.

Anna's call came on the seventh day, but there was no rejoicing. Remo was going to have to return to America and stop Harold W. Smith. He had gone insane.

"He's screaming 'Forty-four-forty or fight,' and he's starting a war with Canada."

"Smitty?" asked Remo, unbelieving.

"Right from Folcroft."

"How did you find out about Folcroft?"

"I told you he's gone insane. He's not bothering with precautions anymore. He's gotten himself a banner and he's screaming that he wants recognition and that he deserves a medal for what he's done and he doesn't care who knows about him. The more, the better. You'd better get back here and save your organization, Remo."

"Arieson?" asked Remo.

"Who the hell else?" snapped Anna.

"I'm coming over," said Remo, who even now saw the great bust of Mr. Arieson being carried on a litter down to the pier with Chiun directing everyone. Chiun himself followed with an alabaster jar.

"What's that?" asked Remo.

"A little pinch of something," said Chiun.

Folcroft was a mess, but fortunately, since it was a sanitarium for the mentally deranged, few bothered to even notice banners flying from its walls. Since it was close to Long Island Sound, many people thought of them as boat signals.

Some of the doctors were questioning why the normally reserved and almost unreachable Mr. Smith was now saying hello to everyone and trying to enlist them in a fight against Canada. They would have committed him to an institution, except he was in one already and running it, and if the truth be known, what made someone a patient at a mental institution instead of an administrator was purely a matter of chance.

According to Smith, Canada had thumbed its nose at America ever since the American Revolution, and the real honest and sacred boundary between the two countries was latitude forty-four-forty, but the cowardly and probably traitorous people running

the country, all Canada-simps as he called them, had
settled for this tragic injustice.

All it needed was for a few brave and honest men
who could not be bought off or intimidated by the
Canada lobby.

Remo gently cornered him with an arm and guided
him back to his office, as Smith very intently asked
Remo if he was one of those who was willing to
forget that during the Vietnam war Canada played
host to American draft dodgers.

"They get away with everything and they control
everything and when you point out these obvious
facts, you're called a bigot. Do you understand?"

"I do, Smitty," said Remo.

"That's why only a purifying war can rid us of this
cancer in our midst."

"Right. We'll join your war, Smitty."

Smith's gray hair was disheveled and his eyes were
wide with the vision he alone saw. He found Anna in
his office. Remo glanced at the drawers to the computer consoles out of instinct. She was not, after all,
part of the organization.

Chiun arrived bringing the bust of Mr. Arieson. It
looked like a kimono as a stand for a ton-size marble
bust. When he put it down on the floor the room
trembled a bit.

From under his gray kimono Chiun took the alabaster jar and opened it. He reached into the jar and
took out a pinch of brownish powder and lit it. Its
purplish fumes tickled the nostrils and made the far
reaches of the room smell pleasant even as it burned
a bright orange at its core. Incense. He had lit incense before the bust of Mr. Arieson.

"O Aries, God of War, called Mars by the Romans,
and other names by other tribes, please do allow

mankind to have his own stupid wars instead of arranging them."

With a whoosh like a storm, the incense clouds were sucked up into the stone nostrils, leaving only a great silence in the office of Harold W. Smith.

"What are you doing here?" he asked Anna. "And you, Remo? And Chiun?"

"We have made the proper sacrifice to the god of war the Indians released on the Ojupa reservation. He's returned to his observer status," said Remo.

Smith straightened his tie and made sure all of the drawers were shut. Ms. Chutesov was, after all, a Russian high operative.

"I don't believe it," said Smith.

"That statue must have some historical significance which activated the electronic waves you talked about, when you tried that machine you had your scientists create to counterbalance any wave coming at it," said Anna.

"Sinanju does have access to electronic forces," said Smith. "In its primitive way."

"Historical forces," said Anna, who had been educated in communist schools.

"The white mentality," said Chiun of both Anna and Smith, as he got Remo to carry the property of Sinanju out of Folcroft. After all, he had personally carried it in. But was he complaining?